THE DARK MADONNA

THE DARK MADONNA

A FABLE of Resiliency and Imagination

Nicolas Bazan, M.D.

STORY MERCHANT BOOKS
BEVERLY HILLS
2013

ISBN-10: 0983605890

ISBN-13: 978-0-9836058-9-8

Story Merchant Books
9601 Wilshire Boulevard #1202
Beverly Hills CA 90210
www.storymerchant.com

Dedicated to those in unmarked graves,
witnesses of how far we must travel to redeem civilization

1

IT WAS LATE AND THE VESTIBULE WAS HOT, CROWDED AND SMELLED of people who had been forbidden from showering. Cruz himself had not showered in days and his own stench was overpowering him. His water had been cut off, not because the bills weren't paid but because the government controlled the water company and was at a point of using whatever means necessary to gnaw at people. There hadn't been electricity in days either. Keep them in the dark and dirty—it was a government obsessed with making everything and everyone exactly as it was.

Family, colleagues, students, and friends of Dr. Alvaro Cruz were packed together like quarters in a roll—stacked. Some were crying while others hugged silently, apparently out of tears. They were waiting for the plane which would carry Dr. Cruz, his wife Elvira, and their five children to the United States.

The family's bags were few, and Dr. Cruz had managed to bring only a couple precious boxes of research along. He hoped his memory would hold out for the rest, for this was before the days of advanced data storage and international access. Everything was being left behind.

No, not everything. Dr. Cruz had friends and the respect of his peers. So they were all heading to a new life, but doing so meant leaving a wonderful old life full of hopes and memories. A language, a culture, a heritage, a full blown identity that having to leave behind felt the closest thing to death Alvaro personally had come near since he watched his aunt seize on the street when he was a boy.

This experience triggered his obsession with the brain, and even more, with the delicate and complex reasons for its dysfunction. He couldn't even bring his books with him. His science books were one thing; he could replace those in New Orleans he hoped. But his books from his days as an undergraduate, the part of him that was private and unseen in his daily activities but was marked in these books as a testament to the searcher he was; not just as a scientist, but as a man.

As a young man he drank up books on philosophy and religion and wrote his thoughts in the margins of Teilhard de Chardin, Gabriel Marcel, Kierkegaard, Camus, Martin Buber, Chesterton, and Kafka as though he were a rabbinic scholar in the heat of Talmudic debate with them. Cruz loved a good argument, especially when the stakes were existential. And these books were the record of his young striving mind, the mind he could not always make publicly known in his career as a scientist. But a mind that nevertheless was still shaping his spirit and showing up in dreams and in what began to feel like strange waking coincidences that bore strange fruit.

His everyday adult mind was given over to details, experiments testing the excitement of a new idea with real quantifiable results. But his mind always craved more. Neuroscience was just one aspect of what Alvaro Cruz was and that's why the Argentine rulers wanted to kill him. If he would just do his science and shut up about it and continue to give the government-sponsored research a good name that would be one thing. But he thought too, as a fully-conscious man.

And Alvaro was unapologetic about this, not from egoistic pride, but from the sense that his personal authenticity was nonnegotiable and there wasn't much he could do but live it out and take the consequences. In this moment he wished he had those old books with him; they reminded him of who he was and they gave him strength, and no matter how internally solid he felt, an external reminder was always welcome.

As everything was being taken away before his eyes he clung to his wife, Elvira, and the five children standing before him. The genesis of his authentic journey, the texts that helped him to debate and ultimately claim his convictions such that he could feel empowered to stand up even in the face of fear, would now be a memory. He looked down at his youngest, innocent to everything that was happening save the smell and the tight space, and he wondered if Ana would ever come to know the country of her birth.

These thoughts passed through Alvaro intimately, and for a moment the stinking place was sacred and he felt quiet inside. Moved.

A man approached suddenly, his eyes fixed on Alvaro as he marched arrogantly with the rulers' endorsed authority of a military man paid to act, not think. Alvaro was brought back to his physical self in total and felt the instinct of fear rise, the quickening pulse, the feeling of the need to protect, to fight to keep his family safe.

Were they to have made it this far only to be taken in after all? Was the last turn of events a trick the rulers played—take you as close to the finish line as possible, make you feel safe and then pounce? The man ignored everyone as he strode forward like the dreaded principal entering the classroom with a scowl, only worse.

The children grew silent, even Ana. He stared Alvaro down as he neared, bringing his face so close his breath burned across Alvaro's cheeks. It was a disgusting smell like none he had ever encountered, and it would be a sensation he would never describe to anyone and that he would never forget. Alvaro would be able to recall that face forever, the pale skin, the patchy beard of stringy black hairs and the dark eyes that held a terrible familiarity with violence.

The man's face twisted. He shouted: "We should have gotten rid of you long ago, professor." Flecks of spit showered Alvaro's face, but he held still, not even wiping them off. There was nothing to do; numbness came over him and the passing of time halted. Behind the man another figure kept his distance. He was costumed in full military garb, complete with a rifle at his side that looked like a prop in some play that had been acted out throughout history too many times with too many confused men settling for these bit parts.

The man in his face was an underling, thought Alvaro, and that could either embolden him or restrain him. One never knew with the military anymore. So many others, like Alvaro, had never even made it this far. He thought of colleagues and friends who had disappeared in the middle of the night, sometimes with their entire families, never to be heard from again. Since the coup in 1976 his world had begun to quake, the ground opening beneath it swallowing up everything that was routine—a fault line that day by day had taken away all the years of his life that had been carefully constructed and planned. First they took away everything he had professionally, and then the threats of death against him and his family began.

The offer from a medical school in the USA was a lifeline, a blessing for him and his family. He pushed away the thought of what could happen if they didn't make it out; if they couldn't get on that plane today. This last week was one breath at a time and that's how he kept it going now, just following his breathing, trying with all his effort to keep the panic at bay; to find that authentic fearless place and respond from it.

The man finished yelling, breathing heavily in the suffocating heat of the small room, exhausted from his own anger. Alvaro continued to follow his own breath, counting inhales and exhales, willing his eyes to betray nothing, no sign of resistance or fear, nothing for the man to react to. Time seemed to stop. A kind of suspension or stalemate. The man reached in his pocket and dug out a small pouch of tobacco and some papers. He rolled a cigarette carefully trying to regain his composure. He asked Alvaro if he wanted one and Alvaro consented, not knowing what a refusal would arouse. The man twisted two cigarettes closed, struck a match and lit them both in his still twisted mouth, now more from tiredness than anger, inhaled and then passed one to Alvaro. Alvaro took a drag without upsetting his already calm breathing pattern. The smoke simply showed an external picture of what had become an even inhale and exhale. Everything else was fading away; only the breathing remained.

They smoked without a word, the military man regaining his composure and Alvaro watching the external gauge of his even breath. Elvira looked on in rapt amazement. The other military man stepped forward, grabbed a pouch and papers from his own pocket, and rolled his own. The three of them stood there like friends smoking after a conversation that had run its course without true winners or losers. These silent five minutes felt like a kind of purgatory; they always would. The cigarettes came down to their ends; the men smoked them until their fingers burned.

The military men smiled the smile of demons eating your soul, patted Alvaro on the head and turned to leave. "Enjoy America, doctor!" they chimed. "Don't come back! Next time it won't be a cigarette we share together!"

Finally both military men were in the distance and their backs walked on out of earshot and passed the point of turning to look.

Alvaro's breath came spilling out uneven and hurried as though he had been able to control it by some magic that had finally given way as if at once it was midnight and the chariot held out just long enough before turning back to a pumpkin. He looked to Elvira surrounded by the children and met a mixture of fear, shock and relief in her eyes. She nodded to him, silently acknowledging how close they had come to the end.

It may have been moments or hours later that the family boarded the plane. Alvaro remembered nothing of how he had found his way on board, or even the many goodbyes which must have taken place. Time continued to swirl and mutate, compressed into Aristotelian dramatic forms. Was it early morning or early evening? Alvaro and Elvira settled their brood into their seats, urging each child to sleep if they could. The children, having been told of the trip only twenty-four hours before, were confused but subdued. They knew something that couldn't be explained at the moment was happening. Their parents' unease, a thing they rarely experienced but had seen often these last months, had silenced any objections to the trip. Sorrow and confusion filled the plane; as though the cabin was being pressurized by it rather than oxygen. The stories behind the sorrow re-circulated from Argentine family to family, each breathing in the pain of the others.

Patricia, the oldest child at fourteen years, watched the only home she'd ever known disappear under a thick blanket of clouds that pulled a cover up and over the world below. Higher and higher they rose, until the window showed nothing but deep blue and Argentina was a vanished memory absent from whatever was present now.

Alvaro breathed deeply, letting the relief of escape settle into his bones. The miracle of their good fortune weighed on him simultaneously with their loss. This ambiguity of feeling would be an almost constant refrain now that exile had come to pass. Many were unable to fly away from the open sore that was once his beloved country; he thought of them being swallowed up by it just as he flew over the pampas and the tears ran down his face, the tears he had been holding in for months as he practically dealt with the chaos coming at him daily. His children knew enough to look away.

Feeling profound gratitude for his children's safety and that of Elvira, he also ached at the thought that he might not see his homeland again for a long time and so many other family and friends. Elvira reached for his hand and he took it as a lifeline to everything he cared about. She was filled with the same mix of joy and sorrow, and the tears streaming down her tired face reminded him to finally wipe his own.

A loud crackle from a speaker woke Alvaro. He pulled his head up with a start. His mouth was dry; he had to swallow a few times to clear the dust in his throat. Where was he? He felt a familiar hand on his and turned his head to find Elvira watching him bemusedly, a fond smile playing on her lips.

"Better?" she asked. "That looked like a deep sleep this time." She grinned as he wiped away a spot of drool. "We're nearly to the camp, so we should get our things together."

"The camp?" asked Alvaro, utterly confused.

"Auschwitz. You really were in a deep sleep this time."

2

THEY WERE VISITING POLAND AND HAD LEFT KRAKOW THAT morning. The jetlag from New Orleans was still on him like a drug. His consciousness rearranged itself and Alvaro felt the years since Argentina stretch out behind him. Was that really twenty-four years ago? He hadn't thought of that farewell in such a long while, and never had he remembered it as vividly as he had in the dream.

Out the window he could see the rich green fields and full summer trees of the country's southern terrain. Poland was hauntingly beautiful, in a way that reminded him of Argentina. Its vibrant greens and striking landscapes were of a different, colder region, yet the land resonated in his body; particularly the people out farming it in small patches. People who owned the land and needed it to live, not workers on a migrant jaunt supporting a company that was making too much and compensating their workers too little, the way so much of farming had seemed to go in America whenever he noticed it.

Cruz was standing now to see out the window and take it all in, a present-time movie to wash away the past nightmare his mind had created under his closed lids. He was trying to flood the memories out with the daylight of the present.

They went over a bump and Alvaro fell back. The conductor shouted for Alvaro to sit down. Alvaro didn't know much Polish yet, but he knew that the driver was barking at him; anger is a universal language. A growl would have sufficed. Back down in his seat, Elvira laughing at him, a young man, who had been rapt in his book, picked his head up for the briefest of seconds and stole a glance at Alvaro. Cruz noticed the young man's book—*Memory and Identity: Conversations at the Dawn of a Millennium*, by Pope John Paul II.

Alvaro had read the same book himself not long ago. A passage returned to him suddenly: The Pope had made an appeal for mankind to regard their freedom not only as a gift but a task. The trip felt less and less about the forthcoming conference in Warsaw. After the dream especially, Alvaro was feeling that this trip, the timing of it and the like was no accident. This was both Alvaro's strength and his downfall; his intuition to explore accidents as though they had an important story of their own to tell. It made him a brilliant neuroscientist researcher, boring through every rabbit hole he or a colleague or student inadvertently discovered. It also made him get into trouble now and again when it came to human relationships. Engaging and trusting those who were better off left to the realm of accident and to themselves.

He had arrived in Poland five days prior to attend a neuroscience conference in Warsaw and present a paper on how to reduce or prevent the irreversible brain damage as well as retinal degeneration that could occur following a stroke or when photoreceptors fail to perform and are at the brink of failing. His recent research into the significance of DHA for vision and in the brain held some exciting potential, and he had looked forward to this chance to discuss it with colleagues, particularly his friend, Franciszek, who was simultaneously conducting similar studies at Jagellonian University Medical Center. Elvira had wanted to accompany him, and encouraged him to take some time for a tour of the country before the conference. Alvaro agreed easily, in no small part because of his interest in the late Pope and his birthplace and of the Catholic heritage here.

He glanced back at the young man again who was packing up as they approached Auschwitz, snapping the book safely into an oversized messenger bag and scanning the view.

The train jerked a bit, and rumbled more loudly as they rode closer into the station. Cruz felt his pulse speed up, still tense from the dream and anticipating a destination that was hell or worse. The prospect of seeing Auschwitz was unsettling; he almost regretted agreeing to the trip today. This was no landmark or monument. It was torture and death. Auschwitz was that place where the Nazis rationalized their greatest death camp efficiency of gassing and burning the old ones and the "weaker" ones and working the "fit" ones to death.

Alvaro didn't want to see it, not today, not ever. But here he was looking at the sign outside his passenger window that named this town with the legacy of death. Why wouldn't they rename the town? Why would anyone want to remain here outside the fence? Do they stay because they're numb, proud, or because they have nowhere else to go? Martin Luther King Jr.'s letter from the Birmingham Jail, the famed testament that hangs in Alvaro's office back at the Neuroscience Institute of New Orleans, bemoans not the active racists but the silent majority who do not overtly hurt the cause of freedom, but rather witness the struggle and do nothing. King said that it was this silent mass that would set free or enslave, this silent mass that guides the hand of history and allows life to be used for good or evil. Alvaro thought of that letter now and the silent mass of Poles who stood outside the Auschwitz gates and tended their small plots of land as the stench of human remains saturated the air they breathed.

How could they continue in silence on the other side of barbed wire? Alvaro had no answer; no judgment. He knew the air of fear and the horrible choices that go with it. He knew there was a universe of feeling behind the silences of those who witness the dark hours of history. He had no anger; it was deeper than that. It was a wound that would bleed forever, something not to be fixed by human hands. Alvaro knew this and without a thought felt his heart turn to prayer.

Alvaro shook his head at the reality in front of him, gathered his belongings, and was jolted by the train's brakes as it pulled smoothly into the Oswiecim station as the conductor called out the name in Polish. He packed away a light rain jacket he'd become accustomed to wearing, and soaked up the sun shining in for the first time since he had arrived. The steady heat outside the station was welcome after the last days of rain in Krakow—it brought out different things in the landscape—things that made him glimpse Argentina again though he tried to let that association go.

He and Elvira had become familiar with a Krakow of wet glistening stonework and countless dripping monuments. Here the arid heat felt foreign, like they were definitely in a new place. Yet here also was the sun, greeting them as they arrived at the gates of death.

Oswiecim, called "Auschwitz" by the Germans, was not a terribly remarkable town at first glance. It appeared to be a medium-sized primarily industrial town now of mundane habits and appearance. Once the tourists were unloaded from the rail cars, the train pulled away and revealed an enormous dilapidated compound surrounded by wire fencing behind them. Alvaro felt the blood rush out of him at the sight; the sunshine wasn't enough to warm him. All was cold.

It stood a ways off, to the west of the town. Alvaro checked the map, and realized they were viewing the much larger camp, Birkenau. The camp waited there, silently and gravely holding its place in history; the Nazis had hoped to knock it down and erase it from all official records. They kept the killing going on too long for that though. In their arrogance, even as they were losing the war, they thought at least they could rid the world of Jews before the Americans got to them; they could do what no other nation had the will to achieve.

Alvaro wanted to turn back to Krakow, away from this place that brought an onslaught of his own past that wouldn't recede.

He was pulled solidly back out of his thoughts by a gang of teenagers noisily moving past him with youthful enthusiasm recognizable in any language. Elvira was already up ahead, following the multilingual signs directing tourists to the Auschwitz camp entrance.

He caught up with her and instinctively clasped hands as they neared the older of the two camps. Its rusted gate broadcast the inscription *"Arbeit Macht Frei,"* Work Makes You Free. Beyond the gate over twenty basic brick structures were lined up with precise monotony, a layout created for ultimate efficiency. One after the other after the other... Even though some of the buildings were falling apart or already destroyed, the camp still radiated a sense of industrial purpose and order. Age had softened its structures, but not their intent of a factory built to serve a finite goal. The rationality of the place was chilling; one couldn't help but think of the engineers and architects, the builders, electricians, and all the tradesman doing their work, taking their smoke breaks, joking with each other, as they built structures dreamed up in the minds of determined and powerful sociopaths.

The mixture of normalcy and terror side by side was making Alvaro's head spin as he contemplated it; he tried to stop his mind awhile but it was tough. As a neuroscientist he knew that the way the mind worked was to try to make sense of new input and make judgments and pose theories about the reality before it. He knew this rational bias of the evolved human mind was a hindrance as much as it was a help. It's what once attracted him to the likes of Camus, Sartre, and Kafka as a college student. He knew that civilization had created absurd circumstances that made no rational sense. The mind was constantly trying to make sense out of nonsense. It was a dog chasing its own tail that would not stop until it got exhausted or hurt itself. It was a lousy cycle and getting out of it, even when he knew he was in it, was tough.

Already visitors were stopping, trying to take in what lay before them. The teenagers continued to move along briskly, still lively in the early morning air. Elvira and Alvaro slowly but steadily made their way toward a building which now housed the camp's museum.

On their flight to Poland, Alvaro had distantly wondered what his reaction would be to this experience. Many told him that it was profoundly upsetting, as was to be expected. Walking into the museum, however, the reality of the camp settled in with slow painful clarity and any thought about it felt immediately absurd; he thought of Camus knocking him off whatever comfort he grasped to as a child.

Possessions from the camp's inhabitants were stacked in large glass cases that he and Elvira peered in like display windows on Fifth Avenue in New York City at Christmas time. One room held seven tons of human hair shaved from the heads of every man, woman, and child that entered the gates. Another room the size of a tennis court held shoes all piled together like corpses. Alvaro noticed the scuffed white hard-soled baby shoes among the men's black loafers and the women's brown lace ups. He felt like he could look at them all day; every lace seemed to be calling to him. Elvira nudged him, as he was backing up the line of onlookers. Combs, clothing, artificial limbs, and other random possessions were in the next case. Again, his eyes gravitated toward the children's clothes and he could not help, though he tried, to think of his own children. There was no chance to avoid the past here. Once again Cruz saw the military man's violent eyes and felt the sweat return to his brow as it had in that small airport. He shuddered at the thought of what might have become of his family if fate had turned against them; if he hadn't taken that cigarette or something else as seemingly non-essential but profoundly consequential. Elvira walked beside him, her hand to her mouth.

He watched her face, seeing the young woman from his dream there still, and wondered if she too thought of how near their escape had been. Alvaro was amazed at the number of prosthetics. He found himself counting all the arms and legs and thinking of 1939 and how hard it would have been to get a decent artificial leg or arm back then and how much people must have invested in them only to be stripped of them in a second so they could be thrown in a pile along with all their gold (even their teeth, dentists were on hand for the pulling), their clothes, their hair, and their suitcases, and everything else but their raw flesh, though they knew that was next. It was beyond all comprehension, beyond what the mind could conceive.

The evil of the 20th century had, in one fell swoop, outpaced the human mind's ability to process its events, an evolution of evil such that human thought, compassion, altruism, feeling, and all the things the mind had evolved to do over 10,000 years no longer applied. Artificial limbs to artificial life—Alvaro's thoughts were filling up the tons of suitcases and hat cases and bags of toiletries in the next room: leather cases made to carry people to new destinations, not to their deaths. Steamer trunks; some beautifully crafted, all just piled there, packed with horror. A horror that Alvaro struggled to leave inside the museum. But it was his nature to unpack things—to lay them on the dissection table and examine them. He was accustomed to examining a diseased brain to try and piece together what went wrong. Why the Parkinson's, the Alzheimer's...but this was too much...he wanted to leave these cases where they were, unopened.

But before leaving the museum, they walked along a display of suitcases, each bearing the name, age, and city of its former owner. Jurgen, Berlin, age 11. Stephen, Prague, age 22. Elvira squeezed his hand painfully and pointed to a small case which read "Anna, Berlin, age 9." But not our *Ana*, Cruz thought. *Our Ana is very much alive and well.* They left the small room, wiping away tears in the sudden and too bright sunlight. He felt heaviness about him and knew that the suitcases were on his back and would be bearing down on him.

Auschwitz continued to lay its history out before them in painfully simple details. Here they saw the cells where prisoners were packed in so tightly they could only stand. Here they found the bunks which held five emaciated bodies in a space barely large enough for one healthy body. They saw rooms with electricity but no plumbing such that the lack of hygiene killed a high percentage of its inhabitants. This was Darwinian Theory taken to a maniacal extreme.

The gas chambers next, of simple concrete construction; the walls stained with time. An empty concrete black box; almost like one of those ninety-nine seat theaters off Broadway. None of it seemed real now. His mind was starting to numb, a different kind of consciousness emerging. So many were disposed of here right after their belongings were taken; he couldn't help but notice the layout for efficient disposal. Now, in the present, the camp was quiet; it let them through its entirety without resistance. But there were signs of attempts to hide it away. Buildings partially smashed, walls torn down, signs of the destruction the Nazis had left behind in the hopes of concealing their crimes.

Alvaro recalled hearing about the testimony of a soldier from Argentina, confessing horrific crimes. He had been one of several soldiers ordered to load people into the backs of cargo planes and then dump them, still alive, into the Atlantic Ocean. Crimes such as those left little evidence behind. Here was an entire facility which could bear witness to the Holocaust. For Alvaro the camp stood for all those crimes against humanity which would never have their own museum.

Through the gas chambers and no more than ten paces away stood the crematoriums, furnaces of flesh whose workers rolled lifeless bodies out of the gas chambers in carts on tracks and stuffed them into coal fired cast iron ovens. The crematoriums were black and stained with ash—they looked almost intact—as if they could still work.

They got outside and were ready to collapse. The young

man with the book from the train sat near one of the gas chambers. His white shirt shone brightly in the sunlight and Alvaro squinted against the glare to see him more clearly. He sat quietly, hands folded at his lap. As they passed nearer to him, Alvaro heard words. "Mother, I am yours and all that I have is yours." The man's voice was soothing and beautiful, filled with compassion and devotion that was welcome to Alvaro after that dark space.

The accent of the man was likely American, though not distinct enough to say for sure. Alvaro wanted to approach him, drawn to his sincerity, but he walked on, feeling uncomfortable about interrupting a private prayer.

By the time Elvira and he had made their way through the rest of camp, they were both fatigued beyond anything that could be attributed to the physical. It was time for a rest and some food. The high school students that had leaped so boisterously ahead of them at the start were trickling out of the camp. Their steps were deliberate and slower now, as the history of Auschwitz settled over them too. The girls leaned together and murmured softly while the boys ambled about more silently, kicking at stones on the path and watching out ahead at nothing in particular.

Alvaro thought of their children and how young they had been when they arrived in the States. They were all grown now; some even had children of their own. He wished they could be with him suddenly, not here in this place though; he wanted to shelter them from even the thought of it, especially his grandchildren. Instead he imagined a family meal of talk and laughter around their table in New Orleans, the children's voices carrying away memories of the dead and the suffering.

Their tour book mentioned a few restaurants, mainly

those found in the hotels or one in a church, but neither felt much like making their way anywhere else just now. Elvira had brought a few apples and some cold chicken salad left over from the day before. They decided to skip the tourist lunch and eat their food at the station while they waited for the next train back to Krakow. Elvira dipped two washcloths from the hotel in the ice water of her soft cooler and draped one over Alvaro's neck and one on her own; this made the heat bearable, the heat which had been intensifying as this longest day dragged on.

"Like New Orleans in August," Elvira said. She then passed Alvaro a chicken salad sandwich wrapped in plastic and foil to keep dry.

Alvaro was silent. He chewed his sandwich without tasting it, another funny thing about the human brain which he had studied and written about. It was the ability of the thinking mind to take precedence over the sensory mind such that you can be hearing, seeing, tasting, or touching yet not really taking any of it in if your thought process was intense enough. After the sandwich, a pint of water and an apple Alvaro finally said: "I wonder what Krakow looks like now that it's dry. Maybe we'll have time to go somewhere before dinner with Franciszek." Alvaro wanted to see the old church down the road from their hotel, anything to soften what he just witnessed. Although he knew it was futile to try and soften such a thing he knew too that he would try. It was another of the mind's deceptions that he studied as a researcher but couldn't help but give into as a human being like the rest of us.

Elvira was more realistic about what could be softened and what had to be tolerated. Women were. "I need a rest and a shower...and some quiet. I need some quiet after this morning. What a place, nothing prepares you..." Her voice trailed off, full of feelings that couldn't and didn't want to find their way into words.

Alvaro almost picked up on those words and revealed his dream from the train, but he didn't dare. It wasn't something they spoke about without warning. He took Elvira's hand instead. He was interrupted by a woman's voice shouting on the platform. They looked over to see a young couple apparently arguing, though the language was unfamiliar. The woman was crying and pushing at the man, who yelled something loudly again and tried to silence her. The scene seemed so out of place in the aftermath of their visit to Auschwitz that Alvaro almost laughed.

"I wonder what that was about?" Elvira said.

"Probably upset that he never stopped and asked for directions," Alvaro grinned.

They both laughed, something they desperately needed to do. Elvira bit into an apple slice and passed the container to Alvaro to see if he wanted more. He didn't.

"She's upset because she says he doesn't understand how much of an impact Auschwitz had on her." The young man from the train was standing nearby. He continued, "It seems she had family here once, and the man apparently said something about letting go of the past—my Hungarian is not that good—but that's close enough." The young man paused. "It's really not how it works, is it? The past sneaks up and all of a sudden it's present—right there like it's happening now—you know what I'm saying?" He looked at Alvaro as he spoke and Alvaro felt his arresting presence, simultaneously drawn to it and repulsed by it. The ambiguity of emotional response at work again—damn cerebral cortex! For every other creature on earth it was one or the other; feeling both these emotions at once was absurd. How do you know what decision to make?

"I know." Alvaro answered without betraying either side of the extreme emotional response that was jumping inside him and doing somersaults.

"This was your first visit to Auschwitz, wasn't it?" The young man stated it as fact more than question, and Alvaro nodded.

"I'm Alvaro. This is my wife Elvira. You are American, yes?"

This time it was the young man's turn to nod, as they shook hands all around. Alvaro was turning to pleasantries and small talk, trying to stir his emotions away from the realness of present time response.

"My name's Stephen. I'm from Pennsylvania originally; though I've been here for a few years now. I've been to the camps many times before, but it requires disciplined mental preparation for days before to get through it. It's near impossible for the mind to let in the suffering that took place here; it is easy to be numb instead. But I think that's a disservice to the dead, don't you?"

Alvaro wanted to ask about the words he'd heard Stephen speak to himself outside the gas chamber, but thought better of it.

"I don't think we'll be able to digest what we've seen for some time," Alvaro said, looking away and moving the cold rag on his neck to his forehead.

"We don't ever really; not with the conscious mind." Stephen's face took on a quiet pain. "It is why I come here."

Something has happened to this young man too, thought Alvaro.

"Please, join us if you like." Elvira motioned to a space for him on the concrete bench. "We have apples and chicken salad, you're welcome to either."

21

Stephen accepted the red apple slices and a half a sandwich. He ate eagerly like someone who knew hunger. "I forget to eat sometimes," he explained. "This morning I was reading and forgot all about breakfast. Same thing happened for dinner last night I think. I didn't even know I was so hungry until you handed me this food. It can be so hard to keep up with the body, the mind, and the heart all at once. You would think they would operate more clearly in unison but they don't." Stephen wasn't expecting a response. He laughed and eased onto the bench with the same weariness Elvira and Alvaro felt. It was something deeper than physical exhaustion, though manifesting as such.

They were all quiet a while in the sun. "I saw your book this morning on the train." Alvaro was glad for the chance to discuss something besides the anguish that lingered around the camps.

"Pope John Paul writes specifically of a deep faith in divine providence. It was his belief that God is present and active in history right now...I aim to preserve that thought but then I come back here and I..." He stopped himself a minute and the silence held.

Alvaro felt a kinship with Stephen. Passion was hard to share with others, and faith, in this place, at this moment, was unexplainable. To try and explain felt like justification, a kind of theodicy. Silence was best. God's silence here is palpable. Science was something else, science was where Alvaro often heard God's voice. Alvaro, unlike the early church leaders, saw no conflict between scientific inquiry and religious devotion. His research was driven by a total fascination with the brain and all it encompassed.

Ultimately it was research into God's mind too; though Alvaro never said this aloud. Alvaro wanted only to talk about faith with this man, something you couldn't do much these days outside a confessional. And it wasn't the time. Elvira was asking about Pennsylvania and the moment passed without time for deep talk. The conversation turned to factual information. It was enough depth for one day and Elvira knew better than Alvaro about how to back off strenuous subjects and lighten the mood.

"I was in Doylestown, at the Pauline Father's monastery for some time. After I completed initial training I had every intention of coming here."

"Why here?" Alvaro couldn't help but prod.

Stephen didn't resist. "It had to do with a vision I had as a twenty year-old art student at the University of Pennsylvania. But you don't want to know about that." He was testing Alvaro now.

Alvaro took the bait like a salmon in Alaska on the first day of the derby. "Sure I do," Alvaro said. Stephen nearly stopped himself anyway but Alvaro pressed him on, grateful for the intimacy, the kind that only happens with nuclear family in the States but was a staple with his Argentine friends.

Stephen took a deep breath and looked away as he spoke. "I came into art school wanting to be an abstract expressionist. Jackson Pollack was my hero. I also loved Rothko and Jasper Johns. I wanted to make authentic use of color, light, and shadow. Materials were important, size mattered, but the subject matter was always beside the point. When it came to art with people in it I was bored. I thought it was below me, primitive. Something to learn but not to use; not for an artist that had an individual point of view. I was in my third year and had avoided my most dreaded requirement, medieval art. I thought it ridiculous to have to study religious iconography in a secular university. But rules were rules, I wanted my degree and eventually I consented."

Alvaro listened in rapt attention, Elvira too, though she also noted her watch.

"My teacher wasn't religious but he had a religious kind of devotion to this style of art. He took us to the Philadelphia Museum of Art when an exhibit of Caravaggio had been put together. He lectured on Caravaggio's technique for weeks before and showed some slides; I barely listened. But in the museum confronted by Caravaggio himself I was bowled over. His depiction of the *Akedah*, the test of Abraham's faith such that he brought his own son, Isaac, to Mount Moriah to kill him and burn him as a sacrifice to God. Caravaggio captured the moment such that that old Bible story came to life at once. It was seared into me like a brand that would mark me as belonging to someone forever. And his Christ on the cross was the same. When I saw it I fainted there on the spot. When I awoke my art teacher was there, and he said: 'You got it now, you see what I mean?' I shook my head yes. Everything was different after this. Color wasn't just color anymore. I immersed myself in the art of the Middle Ages. I studied how the Church told its story through pictures. I began to know why Michelangelo could only truly be understood from a Christian perspective. I took a semester in Italy senior year and studied the Vatican art almost daily." Alvaro was rapt. He stopped chewing.

"Art was not abstraction; it was not only color and light. It was story. It was creation, resurrection, and every story in between. It was the story. I converted to the art, through that art, for that art, just as the common people of the Renaissance were moved by Michelangelo's chapel and the windows and the frescoes of Giotto. I was one of them without all the modern interpretation in between that interfered with a direct experience of God."

Alvaro felt deeply engaged. "Your perception evokes in my mind St. Francis of Assisi depicted by Giovanni Bellini, as the deeply enigmatic 'St. Francis in the Desert.'" Alvaro continued. "I went back to see that masterpiece at the Frick Art Collection in New York countless of times because it reminded me of St. Francis's statement. 'First we start doing what is necessary, then we do what is possible, and then pretty soon we are doing the impossible.'"

"That is exactly what happened to me in Assisi. I not only was moved by the art, but I met the Franciscan Brothers and was moved by them as well—their way of life; their devotion. Like living works of art. After the semester at the University in Rome I joined the brothers in Assisi and lived with them for two years. I painted them and Assisi too; I loved it there. A brother from Poland came to visit and I was moved by his piety. He too had a love of art. He told me that art is a church in itself. He became my true teacher. I wanted to follow him straight back to Poland. But when he found out where I was from he insisted that I go first and study at the order in the States in Pennsylvania and make amends with my family who I had been estranged from since my religious quest began."

"And you listened to him?" Alvaro interjected.

"And made amends with your family…" Elvira said approvingly.

"I did listen," said Stephen. "But it was a bittersweet instruction. I made peace with my parents just before my Dad was diagnosed with cancer—so I was able to be with him and help care for him in the end.

"But in that time my teacher in Poland was suddenly killed. Murdered apparently, but no one knew why and no killer was ever found. After my Dad died I studied three years at the monastery in Pennsylvania and then made my way here to meet the people that my teacher loved and even more so, the art that he loved."

"And what was the art here that he loved?" Alvaro found his brain itching for something to like about this country that at this moment at this place felt only tragic and hopeless.

"The Black Madonna of Czestochowa was his favorite piece. I vowed that I would be near it in order to be near him. Have you seen it yet, by the way, the Black Madonna?" Stephen asked, suddenly remembering that he was actually talking to other people with lives and interests of their own. Stephen was one of those people who could not help his own obsessions, though he would look up from time to time. He was looking up now.

Elvira shook her head no.

"You must go! It's not far. Have you heard about Jasna Gora? The Pauline Fathers, of which I am one now, are those in residence at Jasna Gora and the painting is there. You must go see her." Stephen turned to Alvaro now, the words tumbling out quickly. "The Pope was there several times, surely you heard? He always held a special place of awe for the Black Madonna and for the Pauline Fathers for caring for her all these years."

Alvaro had heard of Jasna Gora and planned on a visit, but Stephen didn't wait for his response, back in his own obsession again.

"Pope John Paul II left quite a collection of jewels and robes for the Lady, when he died. The big ceremony takes place in August. They'll crown her again then, but you can still see her in her divine glory now. Do you know there were 300,000 people there at the monastery when he died? The Pope I mean. The divine light was in each of us that day."

Stephen was lit up by his subject, eagerly leaping from one

word to the next so quickly he was barely able to string them together coherently now. But it was not madness, instead there was something burning in the man—a great belief. *Faith*, realized Alvaro. *Complete and utter faith*, a conversion experience that continued to blossom.

Alvaro thought of Thomas Merton and his seven-story mountain as he watched Stephen reign himself in again, obviously accustomed to overwhelming his audience and trying desperately to hold back, at least for Elvira's sake. Elvira asked for facts about the Pauline Fathers, trying to ground things.

Stephen answered more sedately. "We're Latin Rite Hermits of St. Paul. My mother is Polish, and so I've been aware of the Madonna unconsciously for some time; strange thing is she had a religious experience at the monastery as a child and never spoke of it to anyone, not even her mother. She mentioned it only to me after I joined the Order and moved here. She now keeps a copy displayed back home in Pennsylvania and built a shrine around it. My mother has become quite religious also. She always was but kept it to herself for all those years.

"I didn't truly realize what miracles the Black Madonna concealed, though, not until I came here. Make your way to Jasna Gora to see her for yourself."

The train was arriving. Alvaro felt heaviness in his legs as they rose to gather their food and packs.

Stephen thanked them again for their company and the food. He excused himself and Alvaro was glad of the quiet, though he enjoyed the man's presence in a way he hadn't another in a long time.

"He's still a boy really, don't you think?" Elvira was looking at Alvaro with the same weariness he felt.

"Yes, part boy still. There is something very strange about him.

27

"We were planning to see this Lady of Czestochowa anyway, weren't we?" Alvaro continued. "You made notes around it in our guide book, I think I saw that."

"Yes, maybe tomorrow evening," Elvira said. "Tomorrow needs to not be today."

Alvaro knew what she meant. The Argentine couple boarded the train, glad to be on their way.

Stephen was nowhere to be found.

3

BACK IN KRAKOW, ELVIRA EASILY SLIPPED INTO A LATE AFTERNOON nap while Alvaro found himself too charged by the day's events to relax. His mind raced. The dream from the morning was nagging, and Auschwitz of course weighed heavily. He hated how these things felt connected, and Stephen was on his mind too; the story of his life re-telling itself to Alvaro as a variant path of his. Meeting Stephen today was no accident.

For all his scientific training, Alvaro frequently became aware of the aspect of life which could not be accounted for through any scientific method. The part of life, of living, which called him out from his microscope time and again and revealed to him a larger meaning. He was a firm believer in God's presence throughout his life, and even of miracles having been delivered, not more than a few to his own person. He needed to connect with that larger vision in a concrete form and find an outlet for the churning of emotion inside. He was searching.

Flipping through their Krakow guide book, he happened

on a page about St. Adalbert's church, the same old church he had noted down the street from the hotel. It read:

> Tiny St. Adalbert's on the Rynek is interesting from several points of view. One of the oldest churches in Cracow, it has been around since the eleventh century and its original entrance dips two meters below the present level of the square. Legend says that this little church was erected on a site where Adalbert preached before his missionary expedition to Prussia. The present Baroque look of the church is a result of modernization from the eighteenth century. *Open all day.*

He was attracted to the idea of a "tiny" church, someplace private and intimate he hoped to be. It seemed appropriate also that he should attend a medieval church, one of the oldest, given the meeting with Stephen. Alvaro hurriedly scrawled a note to Elvira before returning to the fading light outside.

Directly across the street from their hotel he could see the churches of St. Peter and St. Paul, among others. He felt fatigued again for a moment, and considered stopping at one of them instead to spare himself more walking. But it was a summer evening; the rain had finally given way and the flowers showed they had made the most of the water. They cheered him on down Grodzka Street. There at the end he found the little church of St. Adalbert, a compact design that took generations of workers to complete.

The building was comprised of small squares huddled together with rounded pillars. Two pillars faced him, one much taller and crowned by a green dome. It was a truly tiny church, but distinctive with two lonely round windows staring Alvaro down as he approached. The walls were incredibly simple, painted a plain white though showing their age by the sections of brick exposed here and there. He quickened his pace, wondering *why this church today.*

Around the side, he found the entrance and headed down a set of stairs. He bypassed the main floor and turned instead towards a museum of some kind. He wanted to understand the history of the place before he made his way to the main altar; it was the evolution of things that interested Alvaro. It was one of the things he loved about the brain's structure. Despite new advances in thinking, doing, and communication, for human beings the old parts of the brain that used to do things more crudely and laboriously and still did in times of stress, stayed around. By studying the brain in its current form you could see the origins of human behavior as well as its current condition. But the structure of the brain kept us human beings humble Alvaro thought; it kept the fear of God in us. We had the capacity to write a symphony and prepare stuffed quail with a cognac reduction certainly, but we were also capable of murder and of being afraid of a bump in the night. We were highly rational and sensitive but also a danger to ourselves, others, and the very planet. This was our very nature and the brain's structure bore witness to this, its pathways of neurons revealing our daily choices to be man or beast. Beast was evolutionarily available to us in an instant; the lower brain formed the base of the higher and in a pinch it was the amygdala most people thought with and not the cerebrum.

As it turned out, St. Adalbert was a missionary martyred while spreading Christ's word in Prussia. Alvaro scanned through the information about Poland's first saint and found among the papers a transcript of Pope John Paul II's speech commemorating the thousandth anniversary of Adalbert's death. Nearing the end, the Pope's words read:

As Adalbert believed, it is impossible to build lasting unity without Christ. It cannot be done by separating oneself from the roots from which the countries of Europe have grown, and from the great wealth of the spiritual culture of past centuries.

Alvaro felt his throat constrict at the simple lines. *It cannot be done by separating oneself from the roots*...But he thought of St. Paul's words also, that it is not in, "the roots but in the fruits of one's experience that one is to be judged." Alvaro thought further of William James and his *Varieties of Religious Experience* in which James took up St. Paul's ancient notion and used it as a modern philosophical/psychological expression by which to assess an individual religious experience. It is not in their fantastic description of events that is to be the thing such faith is based on in the validity of their divine encounter, it is in the content of their actions, the way they live their lives afterwards. Hitler and Stalin spoke of fabulous supernatural experiences also that took them beyond temporal history, but their actions spoke otherwise. Their actions spoke of greed, anger, and hatred, the actions of poisonous minds guided by love of power and devoid of divine grace. There is no true window into a man's soul; there are only actions to be reckoned. Alvaro knew that a mind, on its own, is neutral; it is the will that comprises that mind that makes it sacred or profane. So why would the Pope focus here, in regard to this saint, on the roots of Christ and not on the actions that we take in His name? Alvaro let this question fill him up as he turned to make his way back upstairs to the altar.

The main room was small but well kept. Overhead the domed ceiling was beautifully lit by the skylight, brightly illuminating golden lines reaching upward. Around the ceiling, figures were carefully painted, wearing flowing clothes which also strained to reach the circular opening to the sky. An ache in his neck brought Alvaro back to his place on the ground, and in front of the high altar with its late Gothic relief of the Assumption of the Holy Virgin Mary.

The gentleness of the Madonna, flanked by lovely simple flowers, eased his mind a bit, though his thoughts were suddenly on the Black Madonna of Jasna Gora. Should he feel guilty for thinking of another Madonna in front of this one? The projection of humanity onto the painting in front of him made him smile. It was how the brain functioned though, wasn't it? Even as babies, humans begin to find the humanity in every image around them. Alvaro knelt before the altar and bent his head in prayer. This time, history soothed him and the questions temporarily eased as he felt his heart stretch out to the ancient walls which had welcomed so many before him.

His return to the Hotel Senacki was peaceful, and though night had found its way, the city was still lively and filled with the strength of a warm summer day. He would have to hurry a bit, to be ready for their dinner with Franciszek.

Franciszek had been instrumental in bringing Alvaro to Poland. He was working with receptors related to mechanisms in Parkinson's disease, and had emailed Alvaro about his work on neuroprotection, an area of strong research interest to Cruz and his team at the Neuroscience Institute of New Orleans. Emails had evolved into phone conversations, and soon they found themselves friends as well as colleagues, though they had never met face to face. The conference was of international importance, but also served as a welcome opportunity to meet Franciszek in person. Time had been limited until now though, so tonight would allow them the chance to meet less formally and unwind the thread of friendship over wine.

Elvira was up and freshly showered when he returned. Her voice was animated and well rested, ready for the dinner ahead. He suddenly felt worn from his day, and hoped a shower would be enough to revive him too.

"Did you make it to the little church then?" Elvira called to him as he readied the water.

"Yes. Lovely. I've been thinking though, I'd really like to get to Jasna Gora sooner rather than later. Do you think we can make our way there tomorrow right after breakfast?"

Elvira laughed. An idea not only takes root in Alvaro she thought, it tends to grow into will and action immediately the way the magic beans did in Jack and the Beanstalk. She was accustomed to this as Alvaro worked out the puzzles of the brain, selling off cows for beans and coming home to sing about it. This time she had noted the way he paid close attention to Stephen's words, the way he had stretched like a flower toward the sun to hear the devotion and faith in Stephen's voice. It felt slightly dangerous and she didn't know why. She too was religious and was a Dame of the Order of Malta with Alvaro, the lay order for healers of the sick. But faith was a private matter to Elvira. She took to heart the admonition of Jesus to pray in a closet. Stephen's effusiveness about his faith rubbed her wrong but she kept this from Alvaro.

Alvaro had always been full of questions, about the nature of humanity, the brain, the soul, and most definitely of God from the time she first met him in school. His unbridled passion for all things, including her, enamored her. He had found peace in recent years, more inclined to see God's work all around him rather than the lack of it. But today she noticed the old electricity behind his eyes, not so much a question as a quest, not for an answer as much as an experience. It was the young student she fell in love with all over again and to meet him here in Poland was both invigorating and scary. After five children, a well established career, and even grandchildren now, aren't certain questions laid to rest? Aren't the quests of our youth past history and the present filled with contentment among the ambiguities and complications of life? To do otherwise was dangerous, was it not? These thoughts passed through her mind in an instant as Alvaro pulled her to him and kissed her; instantly taking her mind away from thinking and into feeling.

The shower turned on and she heard him humming as he washed away the day. She hoped he would find what he needed at Jasna Gora. If he couldn't, they might find themselves running all over Poland. She called to him in the shower, making conversation: "What was your favorite part of that church?"

"The painting of Our Lady," Alvaro called above the rush of water. Of course, she thought. This has become the theme now. Stephen planted it like a song on the radio played over again that nestles in the brain and stays there for years unbidden. Elvira didn't ask more questions and Alvaro didn't notice.

Franciszek met them at the *Restauracja Wierzynek*, not far from their hotel. It was a splendid building, like so many in Krakow. The restaurant was known for serving the visiting VIPs, including the first President Bush at one time.

Franciszek insisted on eating there, so they could "luxuriate in true old-Polish cuisine." They met by the large rounded stone archway, leading into the restaurant that took up two upper floors.

Franciszek grasped each of them in a full hug, welcoming them both with such enthusiasm Alvaro and Elvira immediately felt like old friends.

"But you are old friends! We met long ago though perhaps not in these bodies!" He winked and grinned as he opened the door for Elvira. "Come, let us sit and share fine Polish food and wine while we talk."

Once seated, Franciszek spoke briefly to the waiter while Elvira and Alvaro each tried to sort out the menu. Most menus were in Polish, they'd found, and it took some doing to decode the choices. But their friend pulled the menus from their hands and grinned once again. "It's all taken care of my friends. You wait and see. I've ordered ahead so you can taste a real Polish treat. It takes time to do it right, so it will be a little while before it is ready. Please, have your drinks and tell me about your visit."

The night went by quickly, and both Alvaro and his wife found the company of Franciszek uplifting and energizing. They spoke of the conference only briefly, and then talked about the magical city of Krakow with its old roots so visible everywhere.

"It's one of the only cities that came through the war unscathed you know. We have witnessed and absorbed more Polish history than any other city in the country. You will not see so much art or learning anywhere else in Poland either." Franciszek had spent his childhood in Krakow and clearly was a loyal resident.

Alvaro understood his love for the city. It was a remarkable place, where hundreds of years of life had left beautiful reminders of the past. Why should he be surprised that his own past would call to him here as well?

"What about Jasna Gora, Fran?" Elvira smiled as Alvaro asked the question; she could have anticipated it to the minute.

"Ah. Yes, you must see Jasna Gora as well. It means "Bright Hill" in English. Have you heard about Our Lady of Czestochowa then? In younger days, I made several pilgrimages to the Lady. She is a very powerful place for Poland you know; our spiritual center in many ways." Franciszek's eyes turned far away for a moment.

Alvaro took the opportunity to mention Stephen. "We met a young man at Auschwitz this morning from the Pauline Order. He was very much devoted to the Lady as well. I didn't understand much about the Pauline Order itself, he was much too eager to mention the Madonna..."

"They were originally Hungarian hermits who founded the order based on St. Paul, the First Hermit I believe. They were brought here to safeguard the painting, sometime in the thirteen hundreds. I think their focus is mostly on monastic life, with the usual voluntary poverty, obedience, chastity etc. They have been the caretakers of the Miraculous Image for most of its stay here."

"And do you believe in the miraculous powers of this painting Franciszek?" Elvira wondered aloud as Alvaro sat up in his chair alert with that same electricity as earlier.

"Oh yes. If it wasn't for the painting, Czestochowa would've fallen to the Swedes, the Turks, the Bolsheviks, or many other invaders. Always she has kept the city safe. There are several more personal miracles on record, but you'll have to go and see for yourself. The legend holds that St. Luke painted it, on wood from the Holy Family.

"Mary herself is said to have sat for the painting, and in doing so she bestowed her grace on all those who go to see it.

It's not easy to get very close, because of all her pilgrims and visitors. But, you know…" Franciszek stopped a moment and worked over a question in his head before continuing, "I have a friend, from childhood, who is installed there now. He's one of the priests in residence at Jasna Gora and I think you will find him very helpful if you wish to visit."

"Yes, yes that would be wonderful." Alvaro said. "If you think he would be willing to meet us, that is."

Elvira watched him clasp his hands like a happy child just told by his parents that he was to go to the circus tomorrow and then place them back on the table before clasping them again. *He is probably willing to head out to see the painting right now,* no matter that he must be exhausted. It was mysterious to her, how a painting could inspire such feverish excitement in all three of the men. Elvira had witnessed this intense interest in Alvaro many times in their life together. It was the essence of the man, to be driven to seek—whether it was answers to the brain's functioning or to find God in everyday life. He was built to sort out and find, in a way she had never quite felt but admired and feared. It was a quality that produced greatness but could undo what felt like stable ground. She had watched Alvaro do both to their life and she wondered where this was going.

Food was suddenly at their table. So much time spent talking, they had forgotten about the actual dinner they meant to have. It arrived in a large steaming silver bowl smelling of cabbage and meats with mouth watering intensity. The talk quickly subsided, as Franciszek dished out their portions. *Bigos* he called it, and its name held their full attention for the rest of the meal.

"*Bigos* is a traditional Polish dish," Franciszek explained, "which is also called 'hunter's stew.' I'd really like to see if you and Elvira enjoy this dish."

When they began savoring the stew of white cabbage and various cuts of meat and sausages, they knew they were in front of a special treat. Franciszek went on to tell them that there are various recipes, "but here they do it the right way using brined sauerkraut, several kinds of wild mushrooms, dried porcini, tomatoes, and honey."

He went on to share that *bigos* was brought to Poland by the Lithuanian Grand Duke Jogaila, who became the Polish king Wladyslaw II Jagiello in 1385, and who supposedly served it to his hunting-party guests.

As the last plate was taken away, Alvaro wiped his mouth and took a deep breath. His head nearly fell to the table then, as the fullness of his belly and the late hour took their toll.

Elvira was still fairly sprightly, the benefit of her afternoon nap, and she and Fran kept up the conversation until they reached the outside again.

Alvaro listened to their voices happily comparing food notes, and breathed in the cooler night air. It helped to wake him, at least enough for the walk back to their hotel. Goodbye was passed around, and Fran promised to call first thing in the morning with more information about Jasna Gora.

"What did you say the young man's name was that you met today from the monastery, by the way? I'll mention him to my friend, explain a little further what intrigued you about the order; not just the Madonna. He'll like that."

Alvaro told him and Fran began to laugh so loud that it shook Alvaro for a minute out of his feeling of wine and fatigue. "The artist?" Fran shouted.

"Yes," said Alvaro softly.

"I met him a couple months ago; he painted a replica of the Black Madonna for my mother's hospital room when she was dying. It revived her. It is a small world, no? I'll call you in the morning."

This was all too much for even Alvaro. He made it to bed with little memory of the walk, and barely got out of his shoes before he was asleep.

Elvira sat up some minutes more and read about *Kazimierz*, the old Jewish Quarter of Poland. She learned that Fran was wrong; not all of Krakow had been spared.

4

THE MORNING BEGAN WITH A PHONE CALL FROM FRANCISZEK. "Wake up my friend! I have good news for you."

"Fran? What time is it?" Alvaro stretched his legs under the covers, as he tried to emerge from a heavy night of sleep.

"6:30! And you are soon on your way to Jasna Gora, so you better start moving. Waclaw will meet us at the shrine at 10:00. I'll be there to pick you up in two hours...Ok? Alvaro?" Alvaro was wide awake at this point and thrilled by the prospect of seeing Jasna Gora so soon.

"Yes, that's excellent Fran. Thank you. We'll see you outside the hotel then? At 8:30? Very good, I'll wake Elvira."

But Elvira had woken up enough to hear the conversation. "Good morning." Alvaro smiled as she yawned groggily. They climbed out of bed and took turns with the shower before heading downstairs to the hotel café. After a simple breakfast, they still had half an hour to wait for Fran.

Elvira suggested a visit to the gift shop, and Alvaro tried to pay attention to the postcard selections she made. His mind was already far ahead, on that bright hill of Jasna Gora. With only a picture of a picture leading the way, he still felt sure about his destination. Sometime between yesterday morning and this one he had become a pilgrim himself. Auschwitz was in the distance and he wanted to keep it that way. What he was heading for exactly he wasn't sure, but the path was clear enough and it was ahead. Always ahead.

Elvira paid for her postcards and handed one over to Alvaro. "For you," she said.

He flipped it over and found himself staring at a broad boulevard leading up to a tall pale spire. "Sanctuary of Jasna Gora," it said. The boulevard was lined by thickly leaved trees, and the sanctuary stood a long distance off from the viewer. Yet it was the dominant image in the photo.

Alvaro stared at the picture, his eyes thirsty for what they found there and unable to look away. What is this? He thought. *Why does it resonate with me so strongly?* A car honked just outside the glass window, and there was Franciszek waiting, beaming with the same infectious enthusiasm as last night. Elvira waved and they hurried out to join him for the drive to Czestochowa.

As he drove, Franciszek regaled them with stories of the Black Madonna. He had gotten more information from his friend Waclaw, apparently, and was eager to please his guests with the new knowledge. Waclaw had been a resident abbot there for decades.

"In 1717, after roughly 300 years of miracles, the painting was crowned 'Queen of Poland.' Since that time, the picture is usually seen dressed in richly ornamented robes and crowned, though not always the same, as she has several outfits for different occasions. Waclaw has told me that she will be given a new more elaborate set of both sometime this month. Pope John Paul II left an extensive collection for that purpose."

"How exactly does one dress a painting, Fran?" Elvira was becoming more skeptical of the whole affair, as Alvaro seemed to be falling further and further into its lure. She tried to bring the talk back to facts.

"Ah, Elvira." Fran laughed. "I too asked this question when I was a child. But you see there is a panel which is hung just slightly in front of the painting with cutouts where the faces and hands show. Do you have these things in the States? Where you stand behind a piece of wood and stick your head through, to be the strongest man or some such thing? We have these for the children, but it is much the same."

"I see. Yes, we have those as well; but it is a surprise to hear about a revered painting wearing robes."

Fran laughed again, delighted to be able to surprise his audience.

As they drove farther outside Krakow, Alvaro could see more of the countryside. The city gave way slowly to agriculture and small towns again and he was glad to be in it with a different destination. The farmland was cleanly ordered, and each little town was well kept and exuded productive tranquility. So much of the land's history had been violent, as in Argentina, yet here the people seemed to enjoy beauty and harmony rather than continuing strife. How was it that the Nazis and the Soviets had trampled through, yet left the people intact as a culture?

"The land has remained true to the people, even after such brutality. So much oppressive force was used here, and yet I feel only the strength of those who persisted." Alvaro was almost speaking to himself, but Elvira picked up on his train of thought.

"It is different from our own homeland, isn't it? Our land too is rich and abundant, yet our people are still struggling to recover from military rule. There are signs of economic and social problems everywhere, and the memory of the *desaparecidos* haunts each village. The people here suffered so much. How have they managed to recover so well?"

She surprised Alvaro, speaking his very thoughts out loud. But she went on. "Nothing is as exactly as it looks, Alvaro. If you stopped at the next farm and scratched the surface of the soul of one who has survived the Soviets not to mention the Nazis and you would find the same pain if not worse as our people. People are strong on the exterior; they have to be. No one knows that better than us, but don't assume what stirs underneath."

Franciszek was quiet and so was Alvaro. After some minutes Alvaro took Elvira's hand and looked in her eyes the way only a husband of so many years can look.

Alvaro wondered about history's role yet again. The words of Friedrich Nietzsche came to mind: *humanity cannot learn to forget, but hangs on the past: however far or fast he runs that chain runs with him.* What chains held Argentina, and himself, and not these Polish people? Or was this an illusion and were the chains running everywhere? Might it be that you only knew their intimacy in the specific brand of your culture or family—that when you looked outside to others it was invisible to you and yours was invisible to them. But if the pervasiveness was truly so about the chains how could we ever help each other?

"Have you read Arnold Toynbee, Alvaro?" Franciszek negotiated a rough dirt road as he asked.

Alvaro knew him well. "He studied the rise and fall of civilizations throughout history. His main premise is that civilizations arise in response to some set of challenges of extreme difficulty, when 'creative minorities' devise solutions that reorient their entire society. When the Catholic Church resolved the chaos of post-Roman Europe, for example, by enrolling the new Germanic kingdoms in a single religious community it helped to sustain the civilization. When a civilization responds to challenges, it grows. When it fails to respond to a challenge, it enters its period of decline."

Alvaro remembered a quote which had struck him many years ago. "Toynbee said 'Civilizations die from suicide, not by murder.'" Even the Nazi murders could not kill Jewish civilization, thought Alvaro to himself as the horrid blatantly murderous picture of Auschwitz flashed in his mind.

"Yes! And in Poland, there is a great strength of religious devotion as you will witness for yourself soon enough. And it has only gotten stronger in the post-communist era. For a long time it had to be underground but in the dark the roots grew deeper, stronger, and more resilient. They burst into almost immediate flower when the Soviets left and now we are seeing the fruit."

Alvaro had already witnessed the deeply held religious faith of Poland. It made sense to him that the country would be held together more firmly because of it.

Czestochowa was a primarily industrial town, similar to Osweicim Alvaro thought as they pulled up into town. This didn't give him a good feeling but he brushed the feelings off. Fran explained that the communists had wanted to dilute the religious significance of Jasna Gora by making it more work oriented, thereby increasing the development of industry in the area. In the end the city amassed a sizable number of smoky chimneys, but none could overshadow the delicate tower of Jasna Gora and Alvaro was glad to see it.

There it lay before them, its beauty and elegance reaching out across the distance between them. As they drove closer, pilgrims were found climbing the road up to the bright hill, many in monk robes of different orders. The tower seemed to ring out to them, to be calling them home.

Up they drove, through the growing throngs of people, cars, and buses which began to choke the street. Franciszek was not deterred however, and he soon turned away from the large crowd and instead made his way to a small church on the left side of the larger monastery. Here, people were making their way more easily, as the masses were headed for the main entrance out front.

"Here is where I leave you for a time, my friends." Fran pulled up as close as he could to the church and waited for them to clamber out. "I will catch up to you soon enough, once I've made contact with Waclaw. He is eager to meet you both and we should have a fantastic chance to see more of the monastery."

Alvaro thanked him. He wanted to ask just how he planned on finding them amidst all the people. But Fran, in a hurry to move on, didn't wait to hear and Elvira was already getting swept away by the current of people moving inward. Alvaro hurried to catch up, and the car disappeared around the building.

The movement of the crowd carried them directly into the main altar chamber. Most people appeared to be Polish and paid little attention to those around them. Alvaro strained to see ahead, and there—the painting. It was hung among gold and flowers, yet it outshone them all. The Madonna's eyes, even from the distance, held great depth for Alvaro immediately. They caught him and held him as he was moved closer and closer.

The people around him were also transfixed, their hands clasped in prayer and eyes round with the wonder of facing their Lady. Everyone moved toward the altar, vying for position in the front the way children do when they want to get a closer look at the parade going by. Elvira walked just in front of Alvaro, finding pockets of space in the crowd to move forward inch by inch.

Alvaro pressed more intently, and the crowd allowed it by responding with the same gentle push of its own. The group packed itself in tighter and tighter toward the altar, forcing out the space between each body until it felt like one moving connected mass, a brain in unison.

Alvaro was swept up in this without thought for a minute, but then a thought rushed in suddenly, as the brain can't help but do. He wondered if they were also going to run out of air, but just then a wheelchair was making its way through. The crowd parted easily, letting the woman pushing the chair move forward without stopping. The man inside the chair was staring at the Madonna with tears in his eyes, and hands clasped together as so many others were doing.

Alvaro directed Elvira into the space which had opened up in the wake of the wheelchair and they were able to position themselves a few inches closer.

Mass began as Alvaro stood before the Madonna. She was indeed a remarkable figure, but he had hoped—expected even—to be more deeply moved by her.

Alvaro felt greedy and ungrateful to even have such a thought; but there it was, and like all firings of neurons, once fired, they are impossible to put back in their place free to swim about the brain from sector to sector.

There was something missing, or maybe "off" was more the word. It's that part of the brain that knows completion and perfection when it sees it. It's why Olympic athletes can know the difference between the slightest flaws in a gymnast's routine. Our brain has receptors to spot perfection in a ballet, a dance, in sport, and even in art; strangely intuitive as it is, the ability exists nonetheless and here it was in Alvaro's exerting itself to say simply: "not quite, but close."

Elvira was enjoying the Mass, filled as it was with inordinate devotion. Soon the singing began and the crowd's passion grew louder, the notes swelling with their emotions.

It was as if the song carried pieces of the people up to Madonna herself, a living breathing sound unlike any other singing Alvaro had heard. Though it was sung entirely in Polish, the emotion was so rich it seemed as if they did in fact understand every word.

Love, devotion, and faith filled the room as the song rose and fell and then was over. Why was that thought of imperfection present? Alvaro was angry at his brain. Surely it was making a mistake, as our perceptions often do. But why now? Why ruin the moment for him?

Tears were everywhere. Alvaro wiped away the dampness from his own and let out a full breath, a mix of heartbreak and devotion.

The same emotion carried Alvaro through prayer and the Creed, as the group vibrated the meaning through him and the hall. Communion was next, but how could they do it with so many in such a tight space? Several priests came down from the altar area and moved through the crowd as though they were channeling Moses parting the Red Sea. They stood in the center of the room and reached all who passed by them, and the crowd organized itself to allow all who craved the sacrament.

It was again a moment of minds connected as though one,

acting with the ease of one being. This feeling took over for Alvaro and the energy of doubt and resistance to the painting's absolute perfection relented and peace filled him.

After Mass ended, two lines formed on either side of the altar. One by one people passed by the painting, stopping for a moment at the closest point before being directed away. Imposing security guards, in nondescript gray uniforms, made sure each person took no longer than their allotted time.

As his turn approached Alvaro felt his eyes strain to observe the Madonna at each step. There was but a moment each to view her close up and he wanted to try to capture some of the magic he had heard so much about and was now feeling thanks to the collective spirit of the others. Like so many other perceptual feats, perhaps religion too was a team sport in the end; each mind needing the other to lift it up out of its own individual chaos and into a collective transcendent consciousness.

But though the painting was indeed riveting, it was more sorrowful than he expected, leaving him feeling as if he should be tending to the Madonna rather than hoping for a miracle of his own. As he stepped into his turn at the close point, he was able to note two lines scratched down her face. He vaguely remembered hearing Franciszek mention an attack, the Hussites perhaps, but the lines were a surprise nonetheless. The guard motioned the end of his time. Alvaro turned away, following Elvira toward the back of the main room. It was a time too brief; and alone at the close point, the thought of doubt returned.

But before that doubt had a chance to settle again and move throughout Alvaro's brain unchallenged to the depths of his soul the silence was broken suddenly by a loud wailing.

Alvaro and Elvira stopped and turned back, to see a young woman crying and screaming hysterically for help.

They couldn't make sense of her words of course, but watched the scene as the guards jumped to sudden life and surrounded the woman. The guards spoke through their ear pieces and in an instant a dozen or more men in gray suits dotted the room and cleared a space for the young woman and what turned out to be her aged grandmother who had fallen to the ground and was now writhing in pain.

The guards called for a doctor, first in Polish, then in Russian, and finally in English. Others may have been trying to make their way from the outer reaches of the room but long before any others arrived, Alvaro was right there. Even without hearing the English words of the guards, Alvaro knew what was happening. He had seen it before as a boy of eight on the cobblestone streets of Argentina when he walked home with his aunt from the bakery. He had seen it and been left helpless and afraid by it; it was his impetus to study the brain, an impetus born out of terror.

The old woman was having a grand mal seizure and there was no denying it. The granddaughter who had brought her grandmother here as a final gesture of kindness, was now frantic with a fear that only the truly helpless can understand. Alvaro needed no translator.

He went to the old woman and tended to her the way he had long ago learned to do. It was a moment of pure instinct. The old woman was trying to speak but Alvaro heard it as only unconscious gibberish, the brain writhing.

In what felt like a long time to Elvira, who did what she could to help, the seizure eventually gave way to a moment of calm. The old woman was exhausted and she and her grand-daughter were moved to a private space along with Alvaro and

Elvira. The old woman's breathing was returning to normal.

It turned out that the young woman spoke English. She was a law student at the City University of New York and had been living in the United States since she was an undergraduate on scholarship at Columbia. She was back to celebrate her grandmother's ninetieth birthday. The girl's name was Iwona. Her English was near perfect, better even than his own, Alvaro thought, who had been in the states much longer.

"She has not had a seizure like this in many years; she is adamant about taking her medication every day and my mother sees to it. She wanted to come here as part of her birthday. I had never been, so it was important to her that the young generation bring the old. My grandmother is big on ritual and she has been here half a dozen times I think, maybe more. She is very religious and I am secular; I think this trip was to try to make me understand what she sees here. I don't know what happened."

Alvaro took a careful medical history; the granddaughter knew some things but not others. In time the old woman came further around and Iwona was able to ask questions of her grandmother in Polish and translate the answers back in English for Alvaro.

But something out of the ordinary was taking shape in the conversation between grandmother and granddaughter and Alvaro wondered what it was. His medical history questions had been answered, the grandmother was out of immediate danger, yet she was speaking in a tone that had the sound of urgency in it. Her eyes looked worried and full of anguish and tears streamed out of them as she spoke. Alvaro was confused.

Iwona looked on with a mixture of concern and disbelief as she comforted her grandmother and stroked her face, wiping away tears with her young smooth hands that just barely

51

resembled the shape of those of her grandmother's. The gray-suited men also looked distressed and uncomfortable and one walked outside the room and immediately began whispering in his hidden microphone.

Finally, out of compassion for the both of them, and because that's the way she was, Elvira asked what it was the old woman was saying and could she or Alvaro help.

Iwona looked up perplexed and frightened that her grandmother's disorientation would not cease and said simply that her grandmother thought the Black Madonna she saw today was a fake; it was not the genuine article. "My grandmother has been here ten times she told me just now, ten times before today, and each time the Madonna moved her and spoke to her, but today she felt something else," she said. "Not the spirit of God but the spirit of man, man's terrible and unquenchable desire, a desire that has robbed the true Madonna of her rightful place. It was in seeing this, feeling this, my grandmother said, that brought back that long ago dead curse of the grand mal seizure…I have never heard my grandmother speak this way doctor," Iwona said, "I'm sorry."

"Don't be sorry," Alvaro said. Alvaro responded instinctually, the way people do when their aim is to comfort something that they neither blame nor understand. This was crazy talk, or dementia talk, or just post-seizure talk that had no precise medical explanation for its content. Context was one thing about such talk, but as to content, medicine was silent about this subject and always would be; it was a safe position.

Before Alvaro could say more the door opened up and in walked the man in the gray suit accompanied by a man dressed in what looked like high ranking vestments. He was one of the Pauline Fathers. The priest had a head of full silver hair and his face was chiseled marble. When he spoke the marble cracked and the ceremonial mask became human. He touched the old woman's forehead and spoke soft words in Polish and prayed with her. The gray suited men bowed their heads as did Alvaro, Elvira, and Iwona. As he lowered his gaze Alvaro thought he might have noticed Fran just outside the door; but he realized this was crazy and tried to concentrate on the priest's tone of voice since the words were beyond his understanding.

After the prayer the old woman seemed better, calmer. But just the same she spoke at length to the nodding priest. Iwona couldn't help but translate to Alvaro, more out of medical concern than religious devotion, that her grandmother was still speaking about the changed appearance of the Madonna; that it was not the same.

The priest was kind and gentle and showed nothing but concern for the old woman. His English was excellent. He asked Alvaro how long before she would be able to be moved to the nearest hospital for tests. Alvaro told him the sooner the better; other things would have to be ruled out. A gray suit spoke in the hidden microphone up his sleeve and in what seemed like minutes paramedics appeared and brought the old woman away. Iwona thanked Alvaro and Elvira as she followed out. Alvaro gave Iwona his card and said she should make contact if she was ever in New Orleans. Iwona smiled warmly and was off.

Fran then stepped into the room. Alvaro had in fact seen him before the prayer; his mind was not playing tricks, though it may as well have been. "Not exactly the meeting any of us were hoping for Alvaro, but this is Father Waclaw, my boyhood friend that I told you about. He is the abbot here."

"Here I was to give you something of a special experience today, and instead you have given me one," said the abbot in perfect English to Alvaro. "How can I repay you? You have saved this woman's life today."

Alvaro felt silly at what felt like overstatement; any doctor, nurse, or paramedic could have done the same. But still he was glad to do it; to be there. As a researcher in the lab he sometimes lost touch with the urgency of the brain's need in crisis. It is good to be reminded of its connections to the body and soul and to the bodies and souls of others that share a life together. "No repayment necessary," Alvaro said.

"You will stay in the monastery tonight, be our guests at dinner and before any of that we will go back to the sanctuary so you can have more time with the Black Madonna without all of that throng of people."

Though Alvaro thought all of it undeserved he nevertheless appreciated it, especially the chance for more time with the Madonna.

Father Waclaw waved the gray-suited security guards away and escorted Alvaro, Elvira, and Fran into the sanctuary after it had been closed to the public for the day. "Fran has probably already told you the history of the Madonna and this church built in her service, so I won't bore you with more history. And besides which I am not primarily a historian or a tour guide, though I play that role to those not of the faith, so I won't go on about facts. Facts don't interest me as much as stories do. I love the Bible for its stories, not for its facts. How about you Alvaro?" Father Waclaw stood looking at the Madonna, speaking in a reverential tone, the way one does when looking at a breathtaking sunset on a mountain, speaking to others, yet not taking their eye off the shared source of inspiration.

"Yes, the stories," Alvaro agreed.

"But when it comes to the brain, to science, you are more

concerned with facts than stories, isn't that correct?" said the abbot.

Elvira was puzzled at the turn of conversation, but not concerned. She couldn't help but answer for Alvaro. "I don't mean to interrupt, but you are speaking about two different things, Father."

"Am I?" Father Waclaw said, without taking his eyes off the Black Madonna. "The story the old woman was telling about her experience with the Black Madonna today, do you think the story is of religious significance or medical significance?"

"Perhaps both," Alvaro said after a long pause. "As for the religious it is a matter of personal perception, the medical we can look at, run tests."

Without breaking his calm reverential tone of conversation, as though commenting on the color of the sky, Father Waclaw answered: "The church has always believed that there are also tests to run to determine religious significance. This old woman may be important to us."

Why this old woman would be important to Father Waclaw, Alvaro had no idea. But before Alvaro could respond with his next question, which he hadn't quite formulated yet but felt in his stomach, Father Waclaw dropped to his knees, crossed himself, and recited his creed with a passionate and open feeling. The others joined him and rose only after he did. They were all silent together for a while until Father Waclaw broke it with a statement of fact.

"I'll leave you now, dinner is in one hour, and Fran knows the way." And with that, Father Waclaw left them. A gray-suited guard re-appeared. Fran, Elvira, and Alvaro were lost in their individual thoughts and prayers. Alvaro, to his chagrin, felt that same nagging pain from earlier that something about the Madonna was not complete. This feeling would not cause him a seizure or any such thing but it would undermine his prayers and this felt like a blight and he resented it. Trying desperately to move from thought to prayer and allow a greater consciousness to take over he heard the whispering of the rosary in Latin coming not far from behind him. He did not look back but instinctually recognized the tone of voice though could not name it. It could have been an old friend, a colleague, someone not too distant—definitely not a stranger—but who?

Five minutes later Elvira signaled to Alvaro that she was leaving. Alvaro followed her out and as he did he noticed Stephen in his robes kneeling several yards away on a bench behind them.

Stephen seemed to take no notice of Alvaro or the others and prayed as though intimate with the Black Madonna.

At dinner that evening in the monastery Father Waclaw did indeed play the historian in response to Alvaro's curiosities. As a researcher Alvaro wanted to learn all he could about the Black Madonna. Father Waclaw did not disappoint. He began with the legend of the painting, told Alvaro and Elvira about Luke and Mary and how it was believed that Mary had blessed the portrait herself. "Art historians believe the painting is Byzantine in origin, probably from Constantinople. The legend will tell you that St. Helen found the painting while she was on a quest for the True Cross, and then brought it back to her son Constantine, the Christian Emperor of Rome. It was said that Constantine built a chapel for it and it remained enshrined there for five centuries. Much as she served Jasna Gora, the Lady protected Constantinople from sieges and raids. After several thwarted attacks, people rallied around the painting, and declared it miraculous. There is one story of a great fire which consumed the city, except a small section of wall upon which hung—" Waclaw looked expectantly at Elvira for her interjection as a faithful student.

"—the Black Madonna," Elvira said, lacking the enthusiasm that Waclaw was hoping for, yet he was undeterred, winked at Alvaro and went on.

"Yes, the painting," Waclaw almost shouted. "It was through the fire that the darkened tone of the painting is said to have come about—the intense heat and soot of the fire darkened the already olive features to their current shade."

"Is there any record of this, any factual evidence to these legends?" Alvaro couldn't help but ask.

Waclaw was not offended in the least, and simply shook his head. "We know very little of the facts behind this painting. I believe it is part of what allows this painting to be so special. Not knowing can sometime open the way for much greater good than knowing; stories, not facts, give people faith and hope in their lives. The Bible is not a science book and this is why it will always be the world's number one best seller. Don't you agree?"

Waclaw's question was rhetorical and he did not expect his guests to answer. He simply went on.

"The painting eventually made its way to a Ruthenian nobleman and was taken to Kiev, to the royal palace of Belz. In this we do have records, and can safely say it remained there for 579 years. During its stay there, however, the painting was attacked by Tartars and damaged when an arrow pierced the Madonna's neck. You should still be able to see the mark where it hit if you are close enough and know what you are looking for.

"Because of the attack, its owner then, Prince Ladislaus Opolski, decided to move it to another of his castles in Upper

Silesia, an area not far from Czestochowa. Here legend begins again, and it is said as the horses carrying the wagon containing the painting reached the crest of the hill now called Jasna Gora, they refused to move. No one could make them take one step farther, and as they stood around wondering what to do Mary appeared to the Prince and instructed him to make her a home on that very spot.

"Thus, the chapel was built, though not the fortress it is today. Greek Basilian monks watched over the painting for a few short years, before Ladislaus brought in the Hermits of St. Paul.

"This is the same Pauline Order which resides here today."

"I had wondered how a Hungarian based monastery had made its place in the hills of Poland," Alvaro finally interjected.

"Well now you know," said Waclaw. "The painting took its home in Jasna Gora and continued to prevent attacks in its new location and give the people reason to believe that its presence allowed for miracles to occur. Over time the chapel was extended to encompass the increasing numbers of visitors who had heard of its miraculous powers, and then the monastery was turned into a fortress to better safeguard the painting as well as the devoted people.

"One of the most important attacks took place during the Hussite Wars. A band of Hussites snuck into the monastery and destroyed many of its religious treasures. The Lady had already accumulated a few treasures, and they stripped her of those before viciously slashing the picture with their swords and breaking the wood upon which it was painted.

"One of the attackers, so it is said, slashed at her face two times before falling mysteriously to his death. The others fled for fear of divine retribution and the painting was rescued and returned to Prince Ladislaus. The Prince could find no one able to repair the painting however, and in 1434 it was wiped clean and repainted anew.

"We now know that the original was probably done in a mixture of heavy waxes, which would have repelled the paints Ladislaus had available. In any event, the painting was scraped clean, repainted, and brought back to Jasna Gora by solemn procession. The symbolic slash marks still visible on her cheek were left as reminders of this close call."

"As abbot, Waclaw is charged with taking personal responsibility for the painting's safety and protection; it has always been this way in the history of the Pauline Order," Fran said proudly, wanting to elevate his old friend to his new friends.

"What happened to the abbot of the Pauline Order in 1434 when the painting was damaged and had to be scraped clean?" Elvira asked.

Waclaw ran his index finger across his neck and made a sound with his mouth to indicate beheading. "Prince Ladislaus didn't take kindly to it, as you could imagine. You are the first to ask that question, as many tours as I used to give."

"It only makes sense to be curious," Alvaro chimed in, "if the abbot is personally accountable to the health and welfare of the painting, to wonder the consequence when the original is scraped clean."

"But that was the Middle Ages," said Fran.

"Right," agreed Waclaw.

Waclaw's "right" sounded particularly ambiguous. Did he mean, "right" the Middle Ages was a long time ago with a very different perspective on the job of abbot of the Pauline order of Jasna Gora; or did he mean, "right" in a sarcastic fashion as if to say not much has changed when it comes to feelings about the painting. Alvaro couldn't be sure; Elvira later confessed that she thought he meant the latter. Either way, dinner was served and in the tradition of the Order, all returned to silence and the meal was eaten with the sound only of chewing, swallowing, clicking, and clacking.

5

ALVARO AND ELVIRA SPENT THE NEXT FEW DAYS ROAMING THE streets of Krakow and soaking up its extravagant history as best they could. They spent time resting and eating, enjoying stretches of sunshine uncommon for the summer months. From time to time, Alvaro picked up a newspaper in English and read about the news around the world, but much of it seemed distant compared to the richness right outside his door. Soon it would be time to return to New Orleans and he was trying, unsuccessfully at the moment, to gear himself up for the journey home.

Alvaro found his mind returning to the painting now and again over the last few days but he told himself that once he had more familiar puzzles to gnaw on back home the Madonna preoccupation would end. The fact that he did not have the religious experience that many reported having at Jasna Gora was not the Madonna's fault but his own and he would have to let it go. But it was hard for Alvaro to let things go.

Alvaro was having these nagging thoughts just before bed as he put down his book on the Wawel Castle. He had trouble going to sleep and tried to soothe himself by picturing all of his familiar surroundings: at home, in his labs, and at the university; all of his friends, colleagues, students, and especially his children. These connections set his mind at ease and sleep finally came. Elvira had been sleeping soundly already for hours when it did. As Alvaro slept, he dreamed vividly.

This time the Madonna stood before him, real and resplendent in robes of gold, amethysts, and diamonds. Her crown, glowing with a warm golden radiance, was the only source of light. Her face, though hidden partly by shadows, looked even more sorrowful than the image he had seen at Jasna Gora. Her eyes were deeper and blacker now. She stared at him, holding the infant Jesus at her side, and tears began to form, running down her face and streaking the paint. Alvaro called to her, "No!" But water had begun trickling out of her two scars, in drops and then gushing. As he watched the Madonna fall away, she and baby Jesus were engulfed in a torrent of water streaked red, yellow, green, and blue by their paint. Alvaro cried out for help, but it was no use: the sanctuary began to flood. Alvaro was swimming for the door when he saw Father Waclaw and Stephen in a black boat. "This is what happens when you come too close," Waclaw said to Alvaro. Stephen threw Alvaro a line that was in the form of his mother's rosary and Alvaro grabbed hold and was pulled aboard the small boat by the two men. "It is not safe to swim alone," said Stephen. "Better to have a boat rowed by people that know the way." Alvaro had no idea what the men were talking about. He only felt exhausted, frightened, and cold. He awoke drenched in sweat and sat up like a rocket, his heart pounding.

It was almost morning, the sky appeared ready to bloom hazy yellows and pinks. Alvaro looked over the city and then got in a shower. He stayed under the hot water a long time feeling his muscles relax and the tension of the dream ease.

He quietly dressed, left the room and headed out for an early morning walk. He bought the International Tribune and a coffee at the newsstand on the corner and sat down on a bench ten blocks up and took the beginning of the day in like a traveler with nowhere in particular to go. It was always fun to be in a strange city without appointments, watching others rush off haphazardly and routinely. He opened the paper and began to read the usual international news about the war in Iraq, the conflict in the Middle East, the situation in Africa and the usual in South America. Everything seemed far away until he was struck by an article about his own home town, New Orleans! Apparently a hurricane was on the way and New Orleans was in the path—the exact target was uncertain but it alarmed him enough to get him up off the bench and heading back for the hotel.

When he got back Elvira was already showered and dressed and waiting for him down in the hotel restaurant, already one cup of coffee into her morning. From a distance she looked sad to Alvaro and he wondered if she too had read the news of a hurricane back home possibly on the way. He got to the table and sat down and decided not to mention anything about the newspaper right away. Elvira was quiet at breakfast, poking at her eggs and watching the other hotel guests as they moved about. Alvaro ate his sausage with bread and butter, and watched her. She finally turned her attention back to their table, and smiled when he caught her eye.

"Is everything okay?" Alvaro asked with worry.

"I've been having dreams this whole trip, clear, elaborate, realistic dreams which leave me with intense emotion upon waking. I've tried to keep it from you, but I can't quite shake this one..." She shook her head as if to toss the feelings out, and shrugged.

Alvaro felt tingling down his arms as she spoke. What was happening here in this foreign country? Something was being woken up for both of them. "Please tell me; you are always protecting me when I should be protecting you," Alvaro said. "What was your dream?"

"I don't know where we were," Elvira blurted as though in the middle of it, "but you and I were standing on some hill, not Jasna Gora exactly but something like it. We were standing on this hill and all around us were flowers made out of precious metals and stones, though they weren't as pretty as if they had been real flowers. I remember feeling sad to have so many flowers and yet no smell to any of them.

"Suddenly the ground of hard packed earth turned to loose mud: our footprints marked the ground as we walked and soon our marked ground was overtaking the unmarked earth in larger and larger quantities until the ground erupted. It was like an explosion of mud, more like an oil field than a spring; it was a mess and it was covering the flowers. That's when I woke up...I'm afraid." She shrugged again, feeling a little embarrassed for not being able to shake off something that did not actually happen. Dreams were rarely of interest to her, and relating one in such detail felt out of character.

But Alvaro was staring at her as she finished talking, a strange look on his face. He seemed dazed, and Elvira regretted saying anything. Sometimes, for all his careful calculations, Alvaro could become quite reactive about her feelings. She was no soothsayer and tried to reassure him with rational explanations about what she ate last night, her stress about returning home, and the strange light in Krakow.

But by the look on his face there was no bringing Alvaro back from his concern and she felt sorry for saying anything.

"I had a dream of water; I was surrounded by it." Alvaro brought out the article about the coming hurricane, and now he too was afraid. They made plans to return to New Orleans and to keep a close watch on the weather. Elvira and Alvaro stopped speaking about their dreams or their experiences in Poland and focused on the rational reality of the coming storm and how they would get back to take care of their home and the Neuroscience Institute of New Orleans. They would have to pack, get a new flight, say quick goodbyes to Fran and others, cancel their follow up dinner with Father Waclaw, and a million other little things.

In the middle of all of this Alvaro got a call on his cell phone from Iwona to tell him that her grandmother had died yesterday in the hospital and that it had been strange because she seemed to be doing so much better and getting stronger. Odd thing was, she reported, that Father Waclaw had come by an hour or so before her death late in the evening and had spoken to her. Something he said caused her great peace and allowed her to let go. "He was there to administer last rites; it was a beautiful ritual, I couldn't believe the timing of it...I wanted to invite you and your wife to the wake later today."

Alvaro thanked Iwona for the call but informed her of his urgency back at home and as he hung up he felt all the mystery of Poland go cold in the face of the daunting reality of his family and friends, home and work in possible danger.

The news now said that the hurricane had taken a slight turn and was no longer on a direct hit for New Orleans and this relieved them. Their grown children who lived in New Orleans reported that friends had helped them board up the family home uptown and that the Neuroscience Institute of New Orleans had also been seen after by staff. Many were evacuating for precaution; some stayed. All the Cruz children and their families headed inland to Baton Rouge or Shreveport.

Alvaro and Elvira breathed a little easier but still wanted to be home. In the midst of frantically packing for the airport they got a phone call from their airline on Alvaro's cell, a surprise of courtesy. All flights to New Orleans had now been cancelled the man on the line said.

"But I thought the storm was no longer headed that way," Alvaro said.

"It isn't, but the levees broke," the voice said, "and water is pouring into the city, the airport is shut down and so is everything surrounding—Baton Rouge too. We can re-route you to Philadelphia or New York."

Alvaro had a colleague at the University of Pennsylvania that he often collaborated with and he knew there was extra room there for a day or two if need be. A flight was booked for Philadelphia but he wouldn't be able to take off for another eight hours. This felt like eternity.

Alvaro hung up the phone and immediately called his children and friends. They confirmed what he had heard and were outside the city already. He spoke to everyone on their cell phones; the land lines had already gone down and the university server was down too. The children sounded fine and Elvira spoke to them to get a mother's assurances. Their friends and colleagues were also in safe places. The Neuroscience Institute of New Orleans was closed as was most everything.

With eight hours before their flight Alvaro figured they could go to the wake after all and use the ritual to put some kind of closure on this obsession with the Black Madonna and his love of this country and the devotion he had been experiencing. He dialed back Iwona and asked the location and then set off. Elvira chose to stay behind and watch the news unfolding in what was being called "Hurricane Katrina." Alvaro promised to return shortly.

Elvira couldn't believe what she was seeing on the news: New Orleans in the center of world news and she was watching it from Krakow. They had lost everything once and had been taken into this warm and generous city to build the Neuroscience Institute of New Orleans. They had built a home over twenty-four years in New Orleans, become Americans, become lovers of the city where jazz was created. They had to leave a home and lose everything once for political strife. Could it really be possible that they might lose everything again because of natural disaster? This was surreal and too much to contemplate. She was getting ahead of herself, the newscasters always dramatize things to make them worse than they are, Elvira thought as she attempted to calm herself down and banish the thoughts of loss that began to swell up inside her. She shut off the television for a while and tried to read her book.

At the wake Alvaro spotted Stephen praying in back and sat nearby. "Praise God that you are here," Stephen barely made audible to Alvaro. "I hoped that somehow I would see you again. Listen to me: you must come with me right now. There isn't time to explain. Just meet me outside in ten minutes. I'm leaving now." And with that Stephen was gone.

When Alvaro got outside Stephen was driving a Vespa and bid Alvaro to hop on. Without thinking, Alvaro jumped on and they were off, bumping along the cobblestone streets of old Krakow. Stephen drove up the incline past Wawel Castle and into an alcove a distance away from it. Alvaro was sweating in the heat and bewilderment of his circuitous journey. Finally Stephen brought them around to a point about 250 yards from a stone archway. Stephen pulled out a pair of binoculars and looked through them, then passed them over to Alvaro and bid him to look through. Alvaro saw the uniformed gray suited security guards from Jasna Gora. "Why are they here?"

"When you visited Jasna Gora the other day you knew," Stephen said. "I knew that you knew."

"Knew what?" Alvaro questioned.

"The Black Madonna there; it's not the one from 1434. You knew it, the old woman who had a seizure before it knew it and now she's dead. You have to get out of Poland!"

Alvaro was reeling. "Slow down, what are you talking about?"

"The guards over there are guarding the 1434 Madonna in an impenetrable safe under Waclaw's orders. The real Madonna hasn't been at Jasna Gora for the last five years that Waclaw has been abbot. He's paranoid about it, thinks it's not safe for public display and that other abbots, had they had the resources, they too would have put up a copy rather than risk the destruction of the original again."

"How do you know this?" Alvaro demanded.

"Remember at the train station I told you that I had come to Poland because I was inspired by a Polish monk I met when I was in Assisi in the Franciscan order?" Stephen asked.

"I remember you saying something about that, yes," Alvaro answered.

"Remember I said that I never got to be with him here but

came to seek out and honor his memory in Poland, but that he sent me back to Pennsylvania to study and make amends with my parents years before?"

Alvaro nodded and waved his hand, signaling Stephen to get on with his point.

"Well, it was this pious monk and artist that I so admired, Father Benedict, who wrote me of the fraud and confessed to me that under the threat of his life he was ordered to paint an exact copy of the Black Madonna, and that when Waclaw thought it authentic enough he would use it to replace the actual one. I never knew if the feat was accomplished because next time I tried to contact Father Benedict he was dead. I came to Poland to find out."

"And did you?" Alvaro asked.

"I've been working diligently on the techniques of Father Benedict by trying to perfect the image myself to see if a 21st century painter could indeed replicate a painting from the 15th century."

"And?" Alvaro pressed.

"It can be done; you would need a microscope, multiple X-ray machines and special cameras and be a trained medieval art historian to know the truth. Father Benedict was very good and through practice I've seen with my own hands and the eyes of others that it can be done. My own master's work is up in Jasna Gora, the original is in that archway vault. I know it. I'm waiting until I can paint what will be the perfect replica of Father Benedict's Black Madonna. When I do I will find a way to replace mine with his and smuggle his out so I can have an art expert examine it and expose what Waclaw has done, not only by locking the Madonna away, but to my master, that old woman, and who knows how many others."

"Are you really calling Waclaw a murderer?" Alvaro asked.

Stephen turned on his Vespa and revved the engine. "Get on! I rambled on too long. The guards spotted us, get on, NOW!"

The guards were already on their cell phones and looking through their binoculars at Alvaro and Stephen.

Alvaro jumped on the back of the scooter and Stephen took off and drove as fast as the Vespa would go. Four hundred feet ahead they hit a large rock and Alvaro bounced off the back. A few minor cuts and a torn pants leg were all. Stephen zipped around, got Alvaro back on and brought him to the hotel. "We will meet again soon, I hope," Stephen said and took off.

Inside the hotel lobby Waclaw was with Elvira in conversation.

"What happened to you?" Elvira asked.

"He's been out for a ride," Waclaw said calmly. "I came here to check on you when I saw you leave the wake so quickly with someone under so much suspicion; I'm glad to see all you have are a few scrapes."

"Father Waclaw told me that the young priest we met at the train station is a known forger of fine works of art and that the black Madonna is perhaps the latest case."

"I have kept things extremely quiet," Waclaw said, "not even our friend Fran knows, it wouldn't be right. But for some reason Dr. Cruz, you got caught up in the middle of something, didn't you? The thing is that I have believed for some time that Stephen has smuggled the Black Madonna out of the country and brought it to his mother's house in Pennsylvania and replaced the one in Jasna Gora with one of his own master works that he has so deftly perfected."

"And why would he do that and how would he do it?" questioned Alvaro.

"He'd do it by simply telling the folks in customs and his

mother that the painting was his own among the many that looked almost identical to it that he often transported back to the States to sell in museum gift shops and churches to help support his aging mother," said Waclaw. "He pilfered the real one late one night between prayers when my guards must have fallen asleep. As for his motive, it's hard to say. He's an American art student turned monk living in Poland. There is nothing about this young man I really understand. He has never been one of us, that is all."

"I find it all pretty far-fetched," Alvaro said.

"Visit his mother's home in Philadelphia, Pennsylvania, and tell me if that is not the real Black Madonna," said Waclaw.

"Of course it has to be Philadelphia," said Elvira. "Can we not get away from this?!"

"Did you know I was…"

Waclaw cut off Alvaro. "I know, I know, your wife has graciously told me everything. Things happen in a particular way in a particular time and we have to use the circumstances we are given wisely whatever their source. All I ask is that on your way back to New Orleans, during your delay in Philadelphia go to this address," Waclaw handed Alvaro a slip of paper, "and ask to see the painting. I guarantee a line will be formed and people will be claiming the Madonna has healing power. With the genuine icon, it is inevitable. I then want you to quietly get it back here. I could not involve the police and face an international scandal and lose the faith of the Polish people. The country would be heartbroken to know that their Lady sits in an American living room because of a thieving monk here in Poland.

"The retrieval of the Madonna has to be handled with the utmost discretion and I have been praying for a solution to

this problem. And now, for some reason beyond convention-
al understanding, my prayer has been answered; it is you who
will need to get this done as quickly and quietly as possible. I
am truly sorry for what is happening in your city. My prayer
is things turn around in New Orleans and you use your time
in Philadelphia as divine intervention to allow things to turn
around in Jasna Gora and be set right as it should be."

To Alvaro, Waclaw seemed sincere.

Elvira was not so convinced. "This is all too much; it's
time to go home. Can we get to the airport please?"

"Yes we can," Alvaro said affirmatively.

"Just don't forget the reason for Philadelphia…" Waclaw
called to them as they left the lobby and headed upstairs.

"Alvaro, what you need to do is get cleaned up so we can
get to the airport. I don't want to miss that flight. Have you
been watching what is going on in New Orleans? The situation continues to deteriorate. I am worried about our house,
our children, my colleagues, research fellows, our students
and their families, the Neuroscience Institute of New Orleans
and our friends. It is time to stop playing around and leave
Poland to Poland and get home."

Elvira was adamant and Alvaro felt the reality of his life in
New Orleans press in on him as a force a hundred times larger than anything that could be going on here. He stuffed the
address in his pocket hoping to forget it and bolted up to the
room to shower and change for the flight.

The flight back to Philadelphia had a stopover in London
with a three-hour layover. In the airport lounge CNN was
blasting the story of Hurricane Katrina. Things were getting
worse. Water was pouring into the city, the roof was coming
off the Superdome, which was packed with people who could
not or would not evacuate the city in time; others were

stranded in their homes. FEMA was slow to act and there was a sense of desolation and outrage growing at the lack of federal response to the disaster.

The Cruz's began to worry about their home. Looters were on the go. They tried to take a broader perspective and focus on the safety of their family, friends, and colleagues— the assurances that everyone they could think of had been accounted for and was on higher ground.

"Things can be replaced," Elvira said. "We've done it before. We are resilient, we human beings. Look at what we and others did after Argentina those years ago. Look at the Poles after the Nazis, and the Soviets out in their fields making the country their own. And the Jews most of all, with everything gone having the resilience to found a new country and farm there, growing oranges in the desert. What can't human beings do? We lose and we go on. The people of New Orleans have this resilience in their heart, blood, and marrow, I know they do. No matter what happens we will recover and the city will recover."

Elvira was adamant and Alvaro was grateful for her faith in humanity and decision to focus on getting through difficulty rather than being broken by it.

But another something else arose in his mind too, something he was about ready to banish but could not. The thought was simple: everything can be replaced except an authentic religious relic or icon. Or could it?

Most of the time in London, Alvaro spent on the phone with colleagues in Baton Rouge at the Pennington Center. The director there was an old friend and had already made the offer, before Alvaro even had to ask, to host the team from the Neuroscience Institute of New Orleans, offering a wing of his own newly constructed state-of-the-art laboratory. There was also a floor of open office space that Director Jaffe offered to Dr. Cruz and his staff to use temporarily until the New Orleans institute was back up and running.

Alvaro thought this offer was incredibly generous and would work out well if need be for a week or so. He had no idea at the time that he would indeed accept the offer and move most of his staff to the capital for several months until the New Orleans institute was fully back to being operational.

6

Upon arrival in Philadelphia, Alvaro and Elvira were exhausted. Cruz's colleague Dr. Bruner picked them up at the airport and brought them home to his large apartment in downtown Philadelphia where dinner was waiting. Bruner was head of the medical school and his wife, Nicole, chair of the art department. A wonderful cook, she had prepared something special for them.

The couples had met before at conferences over the years and found refuge in each other's company. Elvira and Nicole spoke of their grown children and about New Orleans. Alvaro and Bert Bruner spoke of their shared research out of habit, then got into analyzing the federal response as it unfolded in New Orleans.

After a sumptuous meal and a glass of Nicolas Bazan Pinot Noir, Alvaro began to relax and take in his surroundings. He noticed all the bound volumes on the shelves in the living room were art books. As he unconsciously got up from his seat to browse he couldn't help but be drawn to the section on religious medieval art.

"Do you know anything about art forgery?" asked Alvaro of Nicole.

"It's not my exact area but I have worked with forensic authenticators before. Why?" Nicole asked.

"I thought you were going to leave that alone now, Alvaro. Enough with the Black Madonna, we have other things to deal with now, like our home!" Elvira snapped.

"I was just asking…"

"Do you mean the Black Madonna of Jasna Gora? That's funny!"

"Why is it funny?" Alvaro asked.

"Apparently there is a copy here in Philadelphia. One of my students mentioned it to me a few weeks back. People have been gathering around it in a neighborhood just south of downtown. Someone was healed, my student said."

"Have you been yourself to see the painting?" Alvaro asked.

"No, I did not think much of it, in fact, until you reminded me."

"Would you like to go to see it?" Alvaro asked.

"Why are you carrying this over here?" Elvira wanted to know.

"It doesn't seem like he carried it but that it was already here. Let's all go. It'll be a good distraction from CNN tomorrow and a bit of healing wouldn't hurt," Bert quipped.

"See," Alvaro gestured to Elvira, "just for fun. I know this sounds crazy, but along the same lines, just for fun, do you think you can bring some tools of analysis along to see if it's the actual painting?" Alvaro said almost under breath.

Nicole, Elvira, and Bert looked at Alvaro as though he just turned into a kangaroo.

"I know this is nuts, but the head of the Pauline Order

told me he believes the authentic painting is here in Philadelphia. Don't ask me why, but if he's right I need to get that painting back to Poland."

"What kind of conference was this in Krakow?" Bert laughed. "I knew I should have gone with you!"

Alvaro didn't smile.

"You're serious, aren't you?" Nicole asked with compassion in her voice.

"I am," Alvaro confessed.

"By staring closely at the painting I can do a rough *Morellian Analysis* and look closely at brushwork style and color to give an idea. But if the forger is excellent this won't be enough. I'd have to get the painting to a colleague so it could be X-rayed.

"There is a famous case of a Goya painting called 'Portrait of a Woman' that was seen to be a copy in 1954 when technicians X-rayed the painting and discovered a second woman under the first. The forger was using a painted woman of the same period of a less famous artist and painting the Goya image over it. It was a landmark case. The examiners left the painting with both images exposed so other examiners can see the power of X-Ray diffraction analysis over and above the traditional *Morellian*. But I don't know how we would convince the owner of this painting to submit the work to X-ray diffraction."

"I know," Alvaro whispered, almost to himself. "I know the woman's son who has the painting in her possession. I can tell her that her son asked me to run a test on the painting."

"Did he?" asked Bert.

"His superior did and this is enough."

"We will go tomorrow then…a new research project," Bert said.

"I'd rather look at the paintings at the Philadelphia Museum of Art as a distraction from the news," said Elvira.

"How about we do both?" Nicole smiled. "I'll take you on my favorite personal tour."

"Okay," smiled Elvira. "I could handle that."

After a restless sleep of jetlag recuperation, Elvira and Alvaro arrived at the breakfast table just after eleven a.m. and were served coffee, fresh baked orange cranberry scones, and told to save room for the asparagus, tomato, and cheese omelets Nicole was whipping up in the kitchen.

Bert had been through the morning papers and quickly put them out of sight. "Why don't we agree that we won't check the news until we have had our little diversion today? We'll eat a fine brunch, go south to see the Madonna, then back north to the museum and after have some wonderful sushi at Haru just below the Museum of Art."

"It'll be a fine day." Elvira nodded her head. "A day of recuperation wouldn't hurt. But I'll have to talk to the children first."

"Of course," Bert said.

After a wonderful breakfast the four set off for south Philly. Nicole's student met her at the door of the apartment, proud to show her professor something that she had not yet seen after so often the shoe being on the other foot.

A crowd was already gathered. The student explained that it had been like this for weeks now. Word was spreading about the woman with crippling arthritis who had been cured after six separate visits to the painting. Some were applying the story as a prescription for their own illness. But as of yet no other reported miracles had been known.

Upon entering the small apartment they waited in line to get from the foyer to the living room where the painting was leaned up on a high back chair as though sitting on it like a person. Stephen's mother was nearby as was a box for donations that Stephen had constructed for her well being. It was marked for the "Church of Holy Mother."

Upon seeing the painting Alvaro was immediately struck by it. He felt a pulsing in his chest, a weakness in his knees; lightness filled his whole body. He fainted to the floor.

Bert was close by and broke his fall, helped to bring him back around.

"What happened?" Nicole asked.

"I felt as though I were back in Jasna Gora, but not exactly as it was when I was there. As it should have been. It was like the painting recognized me. Can you look closely at it Nicole?" Alvaro asked.

Nicole studied the painting. Finally she nodded. "Very authentic," she concluded.

"And?" Bert queried.

"To know that for sure we will need the X-ray diffraction test," Nicole said.

"Well so far it passed my test," said Alvaro, "perhaps Father Waclaw was right."

"Perhaps Alvaro, but that is a funny thing to say coming from a neuroscientist. Your reaction could be from the jetlag you are no doubt still experiencing, or from the small dark room, or from pure emotional exhaustion. Let's at least give science her due," Elvira said.

With that, Alvaro rose calmly, approached the old woman and spoke directly. "I am okay now. I am obviously very taken with your son's painting. I know Stephen. I was just with him in Poland. He asked me to bring the painting to the university so some art students can see it more closely. This is Dr. Bruner." He motioned over to Nicole.

"How did you say you knew Stephen?" The old woman asked.

"We met on a bus to Auschwitz," Alvaro said.

"What a horrible place to meet. It bothers me that he visits so often, but he says it allows him to touch compassion more deeply. I was the one who asked him to go there. But once was enough. I was a child in that place. There is no need to keep returning," the woman said.

"You are Jewish?" Alvaro asked.

"My mother was born Jewish but converted to Catholicism when she met my father. That didn't matter to the Nazis, though; they were strict about a mother's bloodline. My brother and I were in the camp with my mother; I survived it barely and they did not. I was only nine in 1945 and had already seen too much. Stephen shouldn't know such things, but somehow he found out. I think he goes back there because he thinks it will somehow keep me alive."

"Stephen also spoke to me about his time in Assisi and his decision to go to Poland to become part of the Pauline Order," Alvaro said.

"Even though you do know my son and are clearly a friend I couldn't let you take the painting out of the house. People are coming all the time now to see it and experience some healing. My son does such great work. I would disappoint them if they came for two or three days to only an empty chair," the old woman said. "I feel responsible for her, and to him."

"You sleep at night, don't you?"

"Yes," said Stephen's mother.

"Well, what if I borrow the painting for only one evening, have a viewing at the university overnight—students love the excitement—then have it back here before sunrise?" Alvaro asked.

"Under those conditions I guess I could not object. But you would have to pick the painting up after ten o'clock in the evening and have it back before six in the morning."

"Is tonight too short a notice?" Alvaro pressed.

"You are fond of my son, aren't you?" the woman asked.

"I am," Alvaro conceded. "He is a special boy. Why shouldn't the students have a look? I suppose they would enjoy his great work too. Be back by ten o'clock."

"A day of intrigue and diversion indeed," Bert hooted as soon as they hit the street. "I'll call my forensics colleague and see that he can set up the lab tonight. He'll be thrilled! He fancies himself a true detective and lives for this kind of stuff."

Within ten minutes Nicole was off the phone and beaming. "The lab will be set tonight! Let's go to the museum."

The foursome spent a fair amount of time in the medieval section of Christian art and studied patterns and iconography under the direction of Nicole's trained eye. They also roamed the impressionist section and the sculpture area. Cezanne and Rodin, as usual, spoke boldly to Alvaro; Elvira preferred the Goyas and Dalis.

After a plate full of sushi and bowls of miso soup the four returned to the apartment for a brief nap before the evening's events.

Alvaro awoke two hours later from what had been a deep sleep. He had had an ominous dream this time. Stephen was on a cattle car waving goodbye. When Alvaro woke he had the sick feeling that he would never see Stephen again. He tried not to put too much stock in this, but it was hard.

Bert drove out to south Philly and parked around the corner from Stephen's mother's apartment. Within half a block of the apartment they began to hear wailing. As they got closer they realized it was Stephen's mother crying. Her door was open and she was on the floor with her head in one hand while she banged the floor with other hand that clutched a piece of paper. Alvaro and Elvira together lifted her up and set her in the chair where the painting had been earlier in the day.

"What happened?" Alvaro asked. "Is it the painting?"

"The painting is fine; I have it wrapped up in my bedroom for you. It's worse, much worse." The old woman handed Alvaro the envelope now crumpled.

A telegram was inside; Alvaro hadn't seen one of them in a long time, not since email and FedEx; he didn't realize you could still send them. It read simply: "Brother Stephen Eliot died last night in a small explosion in the monastery furnace room. You are invited as our guest to a Mass in his honor two days from now." The telegram was signed from Father Waclaw and inside the envelope there was also a $5,000 dollar check and two round trip vouchers from Philadelphia to Poland.

"I don't know how I can live without my son. He gave me a reason to look forward to tomorrow." She paused. "I don't even know who I would ask to accompany me," the old woman said.

"I will go with you," Alvaro responded without thinking.

"No," the old woman said, "you don't have to do that."

"No," Elvira insisted. "He will go. He needs to go. I know this."

Alvaro looked to Elvira in disbelief. "I've been getting the news all day on my blackberry," Elvira confessed. "I know I agreed not to," she said, looking at Bert and Nicole, "but I couldn't help it. The situation in New Orleans has worsened. No one is getting in and no one is getting out. It's a mess and Baton Rouge sounds crazy too with all the evacuees crowding the churches. We're better off here for a few days. Maybe our flight was diverted here for a reason. Maybe you haven't just been playing around; maybe you are here now to accompany this poor mother back to honor her son."

"I'm going to stay here tonight with..."

The old woman finally spoke again.

"Maria. My name is Maria."

"I'm going to be here tonight with Maria. You three take the painting to the students. It is another way to honor Stephen. It's important. "

"I'll stay here with you too," Bert chimed in, nodding to Nicole. "The students know best anyway."

"I'll check the flights for tomorrow evening so you two can be there in time for the Mass," Elvira said.

With that, Maria rose and walked slowly to her bedroom to retrieve the painting. It was as if the life was going out of her. She brought it wrapped up to Alvaro.

"Please have it back early as we agreed," Maria said. "It's my memorial now."

7

Somehow Alvaro felt his priorities were crystal clear. His first loyalty was not to Stephen, not even to his failing mother, but to the Polish people and the thousands who made their way to Jasna Gora, like the old woman, only to be spiritually betrayed. When Alvaro and Nicole arrived at the arts forensic lab, Derek already had everything in place. After a brief introduction to Alvaro he launched into the X-ray diffraction analysis and multiple photographs of nearly every square inch of the painting, front, and back, as well as its framing. Those digitized images were uploaded onto a laptop and projected on a large screen that Derek studied intently, comparing it in every possible configuration to a digitized image of the Black Madonna taken seven years ago at Jasna Gora before Waclaw was abbot. They also used infrared reflectography to recapitulate the image of the under drawing, followed by microscopy to uncover the strokes that handled the oil.

Through a good part of the night Derek seemed on track to declare the two exactly the same. But at 3:48 a.m. something gave way. "There it is!!" Derek blurted out, rousing Alvaro from his jet-lagged trance. "See that corner there; there is a subtle trace of 'Caribbean Blue,' a color that wasn't invented until well into the 20th century. There must have been a trace on his brush that he did not fully wash out from another project. I detect just a few specks here, but the chromatic sensors of this program are flawless; it's what the federal enforcement division uses. Whoever he is, he is very good, but it's a copy." Derek was certain. Alvaro was stunned. Alvaro was sure he was about to hear that his religious experience at the apartment in South Philly had been justified.

Perhaps it had, he thought to himself. What if Stephen was simply a holy person of pure intent who painted his heart's devotion to God with pure heart, mind and hands? Perhaps a devoted action of religious intent can never be a forgery and is always cause for renewal and rebirth not only in the one who does the act but also in the one who experiences it. And what if the Dark Madonna at Jasna Gora now was not an act of devotion, but an act committed under artistic duress by Father Benedict under the threat of violence from Father Waclaw. Such an act, no matter the prowess, would surely be seen as one of manipulation and terror by the true believer—hence Iwona's grandmother—who was extremely pious and had known in her heart the difference between technical prowess and the real Madonna. There had to have been others with strong reactions who did not name them as such and many more others who would simply never notice because their own projections of what they want to see are so overpowering. Stephen wasn't a criminal forger, as Waclaw would have Alvaro believe. He was a pious artist devoted to God, his order, and to his great teacher, above all his mother and the Dark Madonna herself; and also Brother Benedict, who he wanted to honor as well by creating a copy based on personal devotion, not one based on coercion as Father Benedict's copy had unfortunately been. The power of true belief had simply been transmitted through the true believer's brush.

Alvaro and Nicole bought Derek an early breakfast at the local college twenty-four hour grill to celebrate the discovery. Derek was ecstatic about the brilliance of the copy and the detective work it took to find the discrepancy. He wanted to call his friends at the bureau about it.

When they returned to tell their discovery, Nicole diplomatically convinced him not to inform the bureau; letting him know something larger was at stake. She and Alvaro had brought the painting back to the apartment early, just before people started lining up.

Elvira woke up on the couch when Alvaro entered. "So?" she whispered.

Alvaro revealed what he concluded. "Stephen was telling me the truth; it was Waclaw that lied to me. He apparently lied to the world. Stephen did in fact paint an authentic Black Madonna bathed in holiness, he just did not paint the one from 1434. It is important I go to honor him and to face Waclaw. It is the least I can do now. I don't think I'll call Fran in advance to let him know. He'll tell Waclaw and I don't want Waclaw knowing I'm going to be there until he actually sees me. I need to."

Elvira was silent a minute. "What is it?" Alvaro asked. "Fran called me on my cell last night to check on us when he couldn't get you. I told him that you were coming back with Maria to Jasna Gora for the memorial Mass. I was so tired when he called I didn't think about Waclaw. Fran is going to pick you up at the airport. I emailed him your flight information that I booked for you and Maria. You leave tonight at six o'clock."

8

Fran picked up Alvaro and Maria at the airport and brought them directly to Jasna Gora. They were each given their own private guest rooms in the monastery. Fran was more formal than usual on the car ride and disappeared quickly, saying he was needed at home and would return for the service tomorrow afternoon.

The main hall where the Black Madonna hung was heavily guarded by gray suits. Alvaro and Maria shared a meal together in the guest dining room and then they went to the main church hall to pray.

While looking up at the Madonna, Maria whispered to Alvaro, "Stephen's feels warmer to me, is that wrong to say? Perhaps it is just a mother, like that one above us, who loves her son."

Alvaro smiled. "It is the furthest thing from wrong to say."

Alvaro too thought of Stephen's painting as he prayed before this one.

"He was a devoted Brother," the monk said. "We loved him here."

Waclaw had yet to make an appearance, but the Brother assured him that he would meet with Maria personally in the morning one hour before the Mass. Alvaro and Maria said good night and retired to their small but comfortable rooms.

Alvaro fell into a deep sleep. All the travel and turmoil of the last days was wearing on every part of him. He was surprised when the lights automatically switched on in the middle of the night. He thought it an automatic alarm to signal awakening for the first of the offices of prayer. But it was no such thing. He looked up to find Waclaw with his hand on the light.

"Get dressed; we are taking a ride to the arch. My security team is outside the door and will bring you to the car."

Alvaro got up slowly, slipped on his pants and pulled over his shirt. "What arch?" he asked.

"You know the one."

Alvaro got into the car and memories began to flood. He'd made it past the guards in Argentina within an inch of his life, smoked what could have been his firing squad cigarette in the Buenos Aires airport with a deranged army officer, and lived in freedom for twenty-four years only to see everything he rebuilt flooded to nothing—only to die at the hands of a person who was supposed to protect him, take his confession, and give him communion. How did this moment come to pass? Is this always where curiosity leads?

They arrived at the familiar archway in the dark and saw the guards posted out front. When Waclaw reached the door he looked at Alvaro and said simply: "Prepare yourself."

"Is this where I die?" asked Alvaro.

"No," said Waclaw after a long pause. "This is where you bring us back to life."

Waclaw opened what appeared to be the door of a Fort Knox safe. They walked into a multi-roomed air-conditioned bunker. In the first room the abbot led Alvaro to the genuine Madonna: the Black Madonna, in all her splendor, seated on a throne.

Down the hall Waclaw led him to an alcove where two men were in prayer: Father Benedict and Brother Stephen. Stephen looked up at Alvaro: "Now you too?"

Alvaro was too shocked to respond. He stared at Stephen in disbelief.

"Not him too," Waclaw said. "You will all be free today, the Black Madonna too. She too will be free. I'm weary of witnessing seizures of the faithful in body and soul. I'm exhausted from protecting myself, and justifying it by saying I am really protecting the Lady. I have banished her and the two of you, who understand her better than anyone so I tell myself she was safe, and the artists safe that could reproduce her if it is so deemed. I have sinned. I know this and confess it to you three men and beg your forgiveness.

"I sent you to search out Stephen's mother and the painting there, thinking for sure you would be convinced of its authority. I wanted a way out. I wanted to stop this charade. But you found the truth and you have returned with his mother.

"I couldn't face her knowing this. It is beyond... What I have done goes beyond. Fear makes a man do horrible things. I heard of abbots hiding the Madonna here during our country's domination by the Nazis and the Soviets. It's been hard for me to get my head around the fact that the war is over. I grew up in a different time, a time when men did terrible things; even to survive sometimes you had to do terrible things. Pure good was for heaven, not Poland."

"That time is past," said Stephen. "I visit certain places, like where we met Alvaro, to mourn and to remind myself that these things are in the past. We must leave them there and not carry them around silently through the present. If we don't remember consciously we become the memory unconsciously. This is how it works with humanity."

"Yes. It is time to leave the dark in the dark and walk into the light," Waclaw said. "I can never be forgiven for what I have done."

"All can be forgiven," said Father Benedict.

"I cannot believe what I am witnessing. . .you were prepared to make these talented and holy men prisoners. Your prisoners! You allowed Stephen to think his mentor had died—allowed the entire Order to think this of the beloved Father Benedict. And now Stephen. . .this young artist who devoted his life to you—you were gong to banish him too and call him dead to the Order. But not just the Order—to his own mother. In a telegram. You are the abbot of the most sacred religious site in Poland and you lied to an old woman of faith by sending her a telegram that her son is dead, heedless of its possible physical effect on her. I don't understand how you can live with yourself! Perhaps for Father Benedict all can be forgiven. He is a holier man than me. . .but not I. I don't forgive this! I can't. I have seen too many good people disappear at the hands of those in power that feared them. I want you to turn yourself in!" Alvaro's voice rose.

The abbot was in tears, choking on them. He finally got out the following: "I behaved like Cain. You are right. I have not kept my covenant with my brother, with God. I will report what I have done. I will accept my punishment."

The abbot took off his robes, stipped down to his long white undergarment and buried his head in his hands to sob.

"I have nothing. I am nothing."

"You are Cain, except in this version you return to God and tell him that you are indeed your brother's keeper and you repent," Alvaro said. "Our God is a forgiving God. Face Him and your fellow men, your Order, and your country as you are, with the truth of what you did, and you will be set free once and for all no matter the earthly punishment you will endure."

Father Benedict offered a prayer through his tears and the men, with the Madonna in hand, walked out of the cave to greet the sunrise. Stephen and Benedict squinted at the light. Benedict fell to his knees with the tears of a prisoner long locked away without any hope of release.

Long after all at Jasna Gora had gone to bed in a mixture of shock, misery, and relief for Abbot Waclaw's public confession of his crime, Father Benedict entered the sanctuary in the modest robes of his order. He looked like any other monk. He held the genuine Black Madonna in hand and walked slowly to the altar followed by Brother Stephen. At the altar he dropped to his knees in silent prayer. Alvaro and Maria looked on, the only spectators. After what felt like an hour Benedict rose up and handed the genuine article to Stephen. The real Madonna was raised and placed back in its rightful home in silence. Alvaro felt the sanctuary change in size and shape. Or so it seemed. The brain sometimes experiences mood as shape; as physical manifestation. He told himself it was his brain having a feeling; but something in the palpable change seemed objective. It was as though they were all experiencing this together, the church growing in spaciousness.

After the ceremony they walked outside into the starry night and felt filled up by the sparkling light. There was no moon. Alvaro thought they would say goodnight but

Benedict led them into a corner of the courtyard outside the church and opened a door with no handle by removing a stone in the bottom corner. On the other side of the wall was a steep spiral single passage staircase that led down several flights and into a large boiler room. In the center of the room was an old coal furnace used to heat the church. "False idols no more," Benedict said, as in a trance. At the completion of that phrase he opened the fiery trap door and tossed the counterfeit Madonna inside. Alvaro watched it burn.

When the Nazis burned Torah scrolls by the thousands in Europe, religious Jews said that the words of the scrolls flew up to heaven unscathed because words of God could not be destroyed by man. This thought crossed Alvaro's mind when watching the Madonna bleed fire. A strange feeling was coming up again. Something felt wrong. Why burn this? Alvaro excused himself, made his way to the stairs, climbed his way to the top and got out into the night air. The cold felt good and so did the sight of the stars. He realized his breathing was labored and something inside him felt sick. He quickly vomited, then felt better. He looked behind him and saw Stephen's mother, Maria.

"You okay?" she asked Alvaro.

"I guess all the..." Alvaro stammered.

"I didn't expect them to burn it either," said Maria." When you try to burn a memory it doesn't go away, it just sears into you—becomes eternally defined. Maybe that's what Father Benedict meant to do—not to erase but to remember. I'm just so overwhelmed and grateful that Stephen is alive. It's hard to focus on anything else."

"I understand. It's just that burning feels wrong here," Alvaro murmured. Soon Benedict and Stephen emerged from underground empty handed. They were crying silently.

"Where's Waclaw now do you think?" asked Alvaro.

"In custody by now I'm sure. He'll await trial there, no doubt," Stephen said without emotion. "I'm glad that before he left us he had his wits about him to pass the scepter to Father Benedict."

"But how will you two 'come back to life' to a church and people that presume you dead?" Alvaro said without thinking about what he was saying.

"The truth will have to be told again and again," Benedict said.

"And what of Waclaw?" asked Alvaro. "Shouldn't there be something this order does to mark his crime?"

"As for this order," Stephen broke in, "we are not a legal authority. May he have a long life devoted to contemplation and forgiveness," he concluded.

"But he put you in a prison, your mentor in a prison, he was going to leave you there. He told your mother you were dead. Your mother, a Holocaust survivor, he told her you were dead! Are you telling me that you're not angry?" demanded Alvaro.

"Anger is temporary. I was angry. But now, now I'm not angry. I'm just sad that fear makes us do things that separate us from God."

Alvaro didn't answer. This one he'd consider a while. How could he not indulge fear and anger, how could he grow closer to God? He knew it was only through love. But how to feel it in the midst of his city being washed away, in the memory of what happened to his first home in Argentina, to the Jews in Auschwitz, in everything that was wrong with the world. He yearned for Stephen's faith, Stephen's willingness to forgive.

The irony of Christ was His humanity. He suffered and

was persecuted as God. How could one consider this? Suffering and divinity are not separate. God is not separate from suffering. He is in it. He came into flesh to embody it, to show that He understands it.

As Alvaro contemplated these thoughts the child in him mused that miracles would be preferable—an end to suffering by an omnipotent God intent on saving humanity. But Jesus wasn't saving the way Superman saves—not saving humanity from physical danger or hurt. He was saving them from bitterness and hatred. He was embodying hope in the midst of tragedy. Difficulty was always going to happen. Alvaro was becoming resigned to this now. But hope was rising up in him too. Jasna Gora was real. The Black Madonna was real. Everything was...and nothing more than the forgiveness of his Lord and Savior. In Poland Alvaro learned to forgive. Not just others...but the world itself, for being crueler and harsher than his rational brain believed it should be. Jesus came to forgive cruelty through the experience of it. Was there any other way for man?

Epilogue

Upon his return to Louisiana and the aftermath of Hurricane Katrina Dr. Cruz took up short residence in Baton Rouge and continued his daily struggle to understand the brain and its vastness, its mystery, and the painful ways it turned against itself in the form of Alzheimer's and Parkinson's. How could such a marvel of an organ also bring so much suffering to the body that needed it? How could suffering be within the source of inspiration? This was the question of the brain...and everything else.

Alvaro wouldn't settle for a simple answer or explanation. It wasn't his place to make sense of the duality, but to live with it and try and make it better. Though it seemed near impossible he would never stop trying to stop the brain from turning against itself. The Bellini painting came back once more with Alvaro imagining the message of St. Francis:

"First we start by doing what is necessary, then we do what is possible, and then pretty soon we are doing the impossible."

He believed it was what God wanted of him, to heal something abhorrent in nature. The world was unfinished and broken and God wanted us to heal it with our love and will. At least this is what the cabalists of medieval Spain believed

97

under the tutelage of Isaac Luria and his doctrine of *Tikkun Olam.* Cruz never stopped trying despite the odds. Whatever was washed away or burned somehow remained for him in some other form, perfected, just in front of him, atop the bright hill.

Discouragement was easy to feel and easy to hold. Hope was elusive, like a sunrise that is too easy to sleep through. But Cruz was an early riser and caught the sun's birth each morning and knew it was real. Some mornings Elvira would join him with a pot of coffee and look out over the lakes near Louisiana State University in Baton Rouge. "It's beautiful," she'd say. "Even with the loss and the trouble, every day is new, unstuck from the past." And in that moment a great blue heron came to life from a wooden pose on a cypress stump, flapped its tremendous wings in the air, and took off.

Acknowledgements

Experiences I shared and places I visited are the source of inspiration for the development of this fable. My wife and I visited Krakow prior to an invitation to speak at a brain meeting in Warsaw in late August, 2005. We stayed at the Senacki Hotel on Grodzka 51 in the heart of Krakow. Our balcony was decorated with colorful flowers encasing a picture-perfect view of the facade of the magnificent St. Peter and Paul Church across the street. The view alone spurred deep feelings because of the stunning baroque sculptures of the twelve Apostles magically lit up at night.

Walking the day following our arrival, we found we were close to the mythic Wawel Hill, the seat of the old Royal Castle and the Cathedral; and to The Old Town Square. The first evening we had dinner in the Jewish district of Kazimierz at the restaurant Ariel, accompanied by wonderful Jewish folk songs. The memories and pervasive atmosphere that the district preserves brought to mind readings about the Rosenthal Tor, in 1743 the only gate through which cattle and very few Jews were allowed to enter Berlin. The fourteen-year-old Moses Mendelssohn, future outstanding philosopher and thinker, was barely allowed access. A couple of blocks away was St. Adalbert Church. It felt like we were walking through the history of Europe at the crossroads of major developments of civilization.

There are literally over 400 Black Madonnas in churches throughout the world: Our Lady of the Pillar in France's Chartres Cathedral; Notre Dame of Monserrat in Spain; Our Lady of Guadalupe, Mexico; The Black Madonna of the Benedictine Monastery Einsiedeln in Switzerland. But our visit to Poland's Dark Madonna, Our Lady of Czestochowa, in the Jasna Gora Monastery—along with the visit to Oswiecim and the beauty of Poland, and the people of Poland themselves, became the hub of our life during those days and beyond. The Black Madonna's impact on me was a profound, almost inexpressible experience.

I am deeply indebted to Story Merchant Dr. Kenneth J. Atchity, who encouraged me to pursue my goals with this fable, suggested critical improvements, and became my publisher. I am thankful to Chi-Li Wong for her exceptional management of the book's web presence; and to Robert Aulicino, for his cover and interior design. I am grateful to Dr. Israel Goldberg, who kindly read an early version of this book and made comments that helped me reshape an important aspect of the story.

To my wife Haydee, who has forever been the checks and balances of my ideas and my sounding board, and to my children Patricia, Andrea, Nicolas, Hernan, and Maria, who have developed their own views of reality and constantly remind me of the motto of my alma matter in Tucuman, Argentina: "*Pedes in Terra Ad Sidera Visus.*" They now have also given me eleven grandchildren who continue to motivate my life as a scientist and a searcher, and who have also been a source of strength for my unswerving faith.

About the Author

Nicolas Bazan, M.D. has been called "a true renaissance man": research scientist, teacher, mentor, community leader, administrator, author, patron of the arts, and entrepreneur. Born in Los Sarmientos, Tucuman, Argentina, Bazan's defining moment was witnessing an aunt suffer a seizure while walking him to a music lesson when he was a young boy, putting him on the path to becoming a medical doctor and one of the world's premier neuroscientists.

He devoted his life to study fundamental cellular and molecular events underlying experimental models of Alzheimer's, stroke, epilepsy, Parkinson's, traumatic brain injury, and retinal degenerations discovering multiple now-patented potential therapies that slow down those illnesses. Trained at Columbia University College of Physicians and Surgeons in New York and Harvard Medical School, Bazan was appointed faculty at age 26 at the University of Toronto, Clarke Institute of Psychiatry, where he conducted seminal studies on responses of the brain to experimental seizures and ischemia. In the 1970s, he established a research institute in Argentina. In 1981, Bazan joined the faculty of the Louisiana State University Health Sciences Center, where he later established and now heads the Neuroscience Center of Excellence.

Among Dr. Bazan's awards and appointments are the Javits Neuroscience Investigator Award from the National Institute of Neurological Diseases and Stroke (1989), elected to the Royal Academy of Medicine, Spain (1996), elected fellow of the Royal College of Physicians of Ireland, Dublin (1999), President, American Society for Neurochemistry (1999-2001), Doctor *Honoris Causa*, Universidad de Tucuman, Argentina (1999), Endre A. Balazs Prize, International Society of Eye Research (2000), the Proctor Medal, ARVO (2007), the Alkmeon International Prize (2011), and the Chevreul Medal, Paris, France (2011).

Since 1981 Dr. Bazan has been one of the first to effectively promote the ideal that a key for the New Orleans region's future is a knowledge-based economic development. He led by example performing cutting-edge science and displaying a transformational entrepreneurial drive. He was one of the founders of In Site Vision, Almeda, CA (1986), a pharmaceutical company that then did an IPO in 1989 and since is publicly traded. Nationally he was a member of the Cardiovascular Drug Discovery Board, GLAXO (1988-1990); Interdisciplinary Development Advisory Board on Alzheimer's Disease, SEARLE (1998-1999) and Department of Transportation Automotive Highway Safety Initiative (1999-2003) among others. Also he was the Chair of a Task Force on "Research as an Economic Force for the Future," LSU Medical Center, (1988-1990); Chair of Bioscience Committee, New Orleans New Business Initiative, City Hall, New Orleans, (1989-1991); and President, Louisiana Alliance for

Biotechnology, Baton Rouge, (1998-2002). He designed and competitively attracted a grant in 2002 to mentor junior researchers, the first major program of its kind in the State of Louisiana; serving thereafter as a model to others.

For his contributions to create a culture that inspires novel ideas and opens a path for translating concepts into reality—from the lab to the development company, to the clinic to the community—he received many recognitions that include: Role Model, Young Leadership Council of New Orleans (1994); The Alzheimer's Association Greater New Orleans Award (2002); Family Services of Greater New Orleans (Ten Outstanding Persons) Award (2003); and induction into the Junior Achievement Business Hall of Fame of New Orleans (2010).

He is the Founder and Editor-in-Chief of Molecular Neurobiology (Springer), a Senate Member (2009-2015) for Deutsches Zentrum für Neurodegenerative, Erkrankungen (DZNE) in der Helmholtz-Gemeinschaft, a nationwide research program on Alzheimer's disease in Germany, Member of the Biology of the Visual System Study Section, National Institute of Health (NIH) (2010-2015), and Chairman of the Board of Governors for the Association for Research in Vision and Ophthalmology (ARVO) Foundation.

Simultaneous with his accelerating and reward-filled scientific career, his civic and artistic community involvement includes being a patron of the New Orleans Opera, developing some of New Orleans' finest restaurants, restoring and reopening an historic jazz club, creating his own Oregon wine label, and authoring *Una Vida: A Fable of Music and the Mind*, produced as a feature film, in New Orleans; as well as *The Dark Madonna: A Fable of Resiliency and Imagination*—both novels exploring his lifelong intellectual quest to understand the interface between science and religious belief. His goal with

both novels, and others in the planning stages, is to enlist read-
ers in this exploration for a better understanding of the deep
beauty and complexity of human experience.

Made in the USA
Columbia, SC
06 July 2022

62868071R00067